a dream of
countries
where no
one dare
live

a dream of countries where no one dare live

STORIES BY
Louis Phillips

Southern Methodist University Press
Dallas

Copyright © 1993 by Louis Phillips
All rights reserved
Printed in the United States of America

First edition, 1993

Requests for permission to reproduce material from this work should be sent to:
  Rights and Permissions
  Southern Methodist University Press
  Box 415
  Dallas, Texas 75275

Some of the stories in this collection appeared first in other publications: "A Dream of Countries Where No One Dare Live" in *The Long Story;* "Easter Sunday," "Merité des Femmes," and "Displacements" in *The Nassau Review;* "Edna St. Vincent Millay Meets Tarzan" in *The Seattle Review;* and "In the House of Simple Sentences" in *Wascana Review.*

Design by Barbara Whitehead

Cover art: The Waiting Room by George Tooker. From the collection of the National Museum of American Art, Smithsonian Institution. Gift of S. C. Johnson & Son, Inc.

Library of Congress Cataloging-in-Publication Data

Phillips, Louis.
  A dream of countries where no one dare live : stories / by Louis Phillips.—1st ed.
    p. cm.
  ISBN 0-87074-349-X.—ISBN 0-87074-365-1 (pbk.)
  I. Title.
PS3566.H485D74 1993
813'.54—dc20   93-24851

For Pat
Words fail, love does not

contents

a dream of
countries
where no
one dare
live

Ralph Scintella was on his way to
Florida to rescue his parents, and I
was going along for the ride. I had
botched a teaching job beyond repair
and I was looking for the pot of gold
at the end of the rainbow. Unfortunately, before you can find the pot of
gold, you have to find the rainbow.
And before that, you have to have
some idea where the sky is, but I no
longer trusted the sky. I didn't trust
anything or anyone very much. Only
high school friends. If you live long
enough, there are more betrayals than
there are nickels, but there's no sense

1

complaining about it. You cannot change your life because it is your life.

I was going to tell Ralph about the movie *Peggy Sue Got Married*, but I didn't get around to it. You probably know what it's about. It's about how this middle-aged housewife with two grown children goes back to her senior year in high school and views the past through the eyes of the present. She tries to change her past, but she is unable to change anything. Because the love of her boyfriend is all encompassing, I would say to the point of suffocation, she ends up marrying the same person she had married twenty-five years earlier. And so it goes.

It's an old theme of course. There's a Russian novel that opens with an old man standing on the platform of a train station. He's sixty years old or so, and he gazes down the railroad tracks (that ultimate image of our lives—a railroad track with nothing on it) and sighs: "Oh, I wish I had my entire life to live over again. I wouldn't make the same mistakes."

But of course he would make the same mistakes. Wouldn't we all? Besides, the problem with *Peggy Sue Got Married* is that it skirts all the important questions that time travel raises. Time travel is a logistical nightmare. If you change one thing, you change everything, and then you can't become the same person who was in the future to choose time travel in the first place. You would be a different person returning to a different place. No matter how much you change, no matter how many details in your life you change, all you end up with is your life.

All right, so I'm not a philosopher. It's not my problem. My problem is that the woman I took to see the movie—a secretary at the college—didn't like the movie any more than I did, but when I tried to get her into bed, she said she was too upset and that she didn't want to get involved in another bad relationship. She was upset? What about me, I thought. Do you know how much it costs to take someone to a rotten movie?

"But I've got to make changes," Ralph said. He was at the wheel of his Dodge pickup and the rain was falling with something akin to anger. He was driving to Florida to help his parents out of a mess. Or *mesh*, as my seventeen-month-old son would say. The home of his parents had been broken into twice within three days and had been ransacked, all their belongings tossed every which way. His parents were so afraid about what was going to happen next that they alternated sleeping schedules. Sometimes the mother would sleep. Sometimes the father. His father, under severe strain, was starting to crack. "I've got to get them out of the neighborhood," Ralph said. "They've been there too long, and the neighborhood is no good anymore. The other morning my mother opened the door to find a black boy sitting on the front step, holding his head in his hands and moaning. He had been shot in the head. The bullet had grazed his temple. My parents are in their seventies. They're too old to deal with things like that."

"I'm too old to deal with things like that," I told him. It was true. I had known Ralph for over thirty years. We had gone to junior high and high school together, and now, after not seeing each other for over two decades, we had met again.

Sometimes I drove, sometimes he drove, and sometimes we drank, and sometimes we did neither. Put that on my tombstone: HE WAS ONLY ALONG FOR THE RIDE. It was raining to beat the band and the moon was the color of beer, but what does that mean? Beer, like stories about time travel, came in so many varieties and colors that if someone happened to remark that the moon was the color of such and such, he or she was giving the appearance of telling you something when, in reality, you were being told nothing at all. Life was like that. It held a lot of noninformation masquerading as information. Even the Bible was like that. Especially the Bible.

I was thinking about the Bible because the jump seat of Scintella's truck was filled with Revised Standards and a copy of *Voyager*, our high school yearbook. After graduation Ralph had attended a Bible college carved out of the old Hollywood Beach Hotel, and so, from time to time, he sold Bibles. His theory was that the Bible opened a lot of doors that vacuum cleaners didn't. Once you got into the door with the Bible, you could sell your client a hundred other things, including insurance. Ralph's heart was in insurance. Or maybe not. Who am I to judge where any person's heart is? Maybe it was in softball or baseball—the greatest single thing man has ever created. After his wife had left him, taking their three children with her back to Texas, Ralph took to church softball games with a vengeance. One day I came home from a hard day of chasing a telephone operator around the sofa (I was going through a phase where my motto was "only connect") when this yellow envelope dropped out of my mailbox.

Dear Jodie:

Life is still going on. I played softball (slow pitch is a game for old men like me) on two church teams. The other day I got an inside-the-park home run with 300' fences and batted 490 for the season. (.700 for the first half then my legs started killing me—Gotta work out more at the YMCA. More!)

What is your parents' address? What is Ivan doing in Pittsburgh?

Ralph

The letter was the same kind of noncommunication he used to write me when we were in high school. It had a way of telling you something without exactly saying anything. The letter itself was the real communication—the paper, the envelope, stamp, and not the words themselves. I was descending deep into misology. I had heard too many words and had suffered too many betrayals. And so Ralph and I simply picked up where we had left off. I had no one tying me to Charlestown, so I took off for Muncie to land a teaching gig: that's how I ended up riding with Ralph through the Flood. It was raining to beat the band, but there was no rainbow.

The Bible says: "And the ark rested in the seventh month, on the seventeenth day of the month, upon the mountains of Ararat." We know where Ararat is. We can locate it on a map, but what was the seventh month in Noah's time? You see?

4

That's what I mean by language that masquerades as information without really being information at all. The new generation is hot for facts.

God tells Noah the exact measurements of the Ark: "And this is the fashion which thou shalt make it of: The length of the ark shall be three hundred cubits, the breadth of it fifty cubits, and the height of it thirty cubits." Again, how long was a cubit then? How do we know? I had just delivered a brief but unremarkable talk about mythology at Muncie's Junior College (I had just measured my heart and found it two feet short of a mile). As I was talking along, trying to stem the flow of utter babble, I—seated behind a desk in order to keep considerable distance between me and the world—I reached down and lifted my pants leg slightly so I could scratch my shin. When I pulled my hand away, my fingers were covered with blood. I kept on talking as if nothing had happened, but I could tell I was in deep trouble. Not with the students. They were wired out of their skulls. They were more interested in The Monkees than they were in the adventures of Utnapishtim and the fine differences that existed between Noah's two of every kind of clean animals and his seven of every kind of unclean animals. I had asked one of the students what he thought the difference was and he replied that the clean animals were virgins, and the unclean animals were whores. It took considerable restraint on my part to keep from performing a human sacrifice.

It was not the students, however, who were on my case. A couple of faculty members were hell-bent on preserving their infertile but income-producing territory. I myself had just come off a championship bout with drugs and had misplaced a wife and a couple of kids in the process. Thus I needed to make more than a negative impression upon a potential employer. Unfortunately my leg wouldn't stop bleeding. Had someone shot me? It certainly seemed that way. My gray pants were soaked. Between the ankle and the knee, blotches of wet dark blood, no ichor this, appeared. It was weird, as if Fate were taking me by the hand and leading me further and further from myself. I tried to put the blood and other thoughts out of mind, though even if I had been in the mood to concentrate (concentration not being my strong point) and could have pulled the lecture back together and spliced together three coherent sentences—even if I could have done all that, the bored academicians slouched in the back of the room like so much gravy would still have held my lack of scholarship against me. I was no scholar, I wanted to shout. No scholar, but I could keep this class from rioting. Were they going to turn me out on the streets to starve? How dare they! Of course it wasn't exactly a case of publish or perish. I had published and I had perished. Let moralists make of that what they will. My one book, *The Anatomy of Hell,* had long gone out of print. GOOP. An appropriate acronym if there ever was one. *Gone Out Of Print.*

I rubbed my nose vigorously and tasted the blood, and continued to lecture the class of sophomores, who carried into the Dolce Vita a combined IQ of 38 (that is, if the inventors of the IQ test granted ten points for possessing obscene skills with bubble gum). One girl pulled pink gum from her mouth, played her tongue upon it, and snapped it back with vengeance. I wanted her tongue in my mouth. A piece of the gravy in the back of the classroom wrote something down. Was I bleeding to death? Alas, the gum disappeared into a great cavern of capped teeth.

"About Manu," I continued. Outside, Adad the God of the Storm was beckoning for me to place my head between my legs and die, but I refused to stop. "Manu, the flood hero from India, had saved a small fish. The small fish had spoken to Manu, cried out to be saved. Manu showed pity on the flounder or whatever it was. Manu took the fish into his hands and placed it into a stream, but the fish kept growing and growing until it was too large for the stream. The fish asked Manu to take him to the lake. Manu sighed, but he showed further compassion. He carried the fish into the lake but the fish kept growing and growing, and soon it was too large for the lake. Manu carried the fish to the sea. Manu, by this time, wished that he had never seen the fish. Soon the fish grew even too large for the ocean, and he warned Manu that a great flood was on the way. He told Manu to build a large boat and put his family on board, and so Manu did as he was told. He climbed into his ark, and the giant fish pulled the boat through the swirling waters and saved Manu from destruction. The fish, of course, was a god in disguise. For some reason gods have to put on disguises when coming to earth. Gods, unlike college teachers, rarely show themselves in all their glory." NO LAUGHTER.

"Even Moses," said a black boy in the second row. "God appears to Moses as a burning bush."

I wanted to kiss him. A response. A human making contact, an effort to establish a relationship. "Yes," I said, "the burning bush. But the point I'm trying to make is that the story of Noah and the Flood which all of you know is not the only flood myth we have record of. Nor is it the first. You should note the parallels that exist between the Noah story and the story of the flood given in *The Epic of Gilgamesh.*"

No one asked me to spell Gilgamesh. I picked up a piece of yellow chalk and my hands were covered with blood. Perhaps my life was blending into the Allegorical and the Anagogical at the same time. Were all our hands covered with blood? Or was it merely a superficial wound? I was always scratching old wounds and opening them. I threw in the towel, staggered to a phone booth, and called Ralph. A member or two of the 12-Credit-Gravy-Train slapped me on the back and offered thanks, but their cheer was a false cheer, cheer that emanated from neither the Gates of Horn, nor the Gates of Ivory, but more from the Gates of Plastic. Don't Leave Home Without It. Too much false enthusiasm, even for me, who had not heard a kind word in more than a year of sweats, shakes, and vomit.

Ralph came to the rescue. He was the kind of person born to ride to the rescue. All you needed was a quarter to make the phone call. Or a charge card. Whichever came first.

Ralph and I had been schoolmates, had met in eighth grade in Hollywood, Florida, and together had written a teenage quiz column for the local paper. What impressed me most about Ralph was his hunger to learn. A few hours after I met him, he told me he had saved his paper-route money to buy a telescope and set of encyclopedias. Ralph wanted to look at the stars. The Cosmos. The worlds over our heads. He had rigged up his camera to take pictures of the moon, but his drugstore snapshots were pathetic to behold. The moon was too far away. In the pictures it was merely a blotch surrounded by a sea of blackness. How could one be certain that anything so far away really existed? The moon was a plot by the Russians to take our minds off troubles on this earth. Still, Ralph persisted at his tasks. He went about his picture-taking with the earnestness of a monk, and every Sunday he played softball for the Presbyterians, returning to school on Monday with tales of astronomical batting averages, savage home runs, late-inning heroics. He was a much better baseball player than I could ever be. His home runs flew over the schoolhouse roof searching for missing planets.

Once he showed me a notebook and inside was an essay he had copied out: "The Most Important Thing in the World," an address delivered by the scientist R. A. Millikan at the National Museum in Washington, D.C. In eighth grade I didn't know who R. A. Millikan was, but his identification didn't matter. I was impressed by the title and by the fact that Ralph had taken time to write it out. The Most Important Thing in the World. What could be greater than that?

THE MOST IMPORTANT THING IN THE WORLD—From my point of view there are two things of immense importance in this world, two ideas or beliefs upon which, in the analysis, the weal or woe of the race depends, and I am not going to say that belief in the possibilities of scientific progress is the most important. The most important thing in the world is a belief in the reality of moral and spiritual values. It was because we lost that belief that the world war came, and if we do not find a way to strengthen that belief, then science is of no value. But, on the other hand, it is also true that even with that belief there is little hope of progress except through its twin sister, only second in importance, namely, belief in the spirit and the method of GALILEO, of NEWTON, of FARADAY, and the other great builders of this modern scientific age, this age of the understanding and the control of nature, upon which let us hope we are just entering. For while a starving man may indeed be extremely happy, it is certain that he can not be happy very long. So long as man is a physical being, his spiritual and his physical well-being can not be disentangled. No efforts toward social readjustments or toward the redistribution of wealth have one thousandth as large a chance of contributing to human well-being as have the efforts of the physicist, the chemist, and the biologist toward the better understanding of the better control of nature. (University of Chicago)

R. A. Millikan

I copied it myself into a black-and-white composition book that eventually got lost. There is a place where all lost objects, words, and people go, but alas, nobody knows where it is. In Roumania, in days of unenlightenment, people believed that when something was missing the Devil had placed his tail upon it.

Thirty years later I wanted to tell Ralph that I thought the most important thing in the world is the way people hold their lives together, but I didn't. It didn't sound right coming from me. I wasn't his teacher. Besides I had nothing to teach. I merely put my head back and listened to the rain. The Flood was coming and we had made our escape.

In the jump seat of Ralph's Dodge, in addition to stacks of Revised Standard Versions of the Bible, there were cartons of green New Testaments that Gideons hand out on street corners. In the flatbed, covered by plastic, were a few miscellaneous items Ralph had purchased from a salesman from St. Louis. Personally, I don't trust anybody from St. Louis. People who root for the Cardinals are losers, though not the same kind of losers people are who root for the Red Sox. But I was tired of being a loser. Of course what was I going to do about it? My life was in the hands of the gods, and the gods were growing exceedingly careless. They were dropping things left and right.

Ralph told me the man from St. Louis was the Greatest Salesman in the World. From the junk he managed to unload upon Ralph, I was inclined to agree. Ralph had purchased two dozen movie posters featuring Rita Hayworth as a blonde saying, "I told you . . . you know nothing about wickedness," three copies of a long-ago bestseller called *In His Footsteps,* a gross of green-paper note pads, a gross of ball-point pens bearing the insignia of the New York Yankees (thank God!), and a wooden leg. The man had more than one wooden leg to sell, but he could only convince Ralph (who had, relatively speaking, two good legs) to take merely one. The fact that Ralph had met his sweet-talker in the Windjammer Bar off Whitney and Houston one evening, with Ralph getting looped and crying into his beer over the desertion of his wife and the loss of his three kids, might well explain how he, a relatively bright man, might buy a trunkload of stuff he didn't need. I wasn't going to allow his lapse to go unmarked, though I too had a lifeful of crap I didn't need.

"He must have been one helluva salesman," I told him. "What are you planning to do with all that stuff? If I were you I would stand on a street corner with a sign around my neck— 'Hey! Look at me. I'm a sucker for anything you want to sell me.'"

"I'm not a sucker," Ralph said. We had been driving on defense mechanisms for the last thousand miles, and we refused to let go of each other's wounds.

"So what are you going to do with a wooden leg?" I asked. We started to smoke. We needed something to relax. My dreams had been getting weird. I was back in graduate school and was working on a dissertation on *Beowulf.* My dissertation advisor was out to get me. A couple of friends had risen to my defense, but it was too little too late, and pretty soon I was swinging across the room on a vine. And then I realized that the professor was queer and his young protégé entered singing "Cherry ripe, cherry." And then I was sitting with my then wife in some kind of auditorium and the professor's protégé was wearing a toga and his genitals were showing, and my wife possessed the good grace not to comment. So there were my dissertation professor and his young lover dancing around singing "Cherry ripe, cherry ripe," and they were trying to keep me in school another year because the administration needed the enrollment and the money, and besides they had taken my money from me under false pretenses since there were no jobs anyway. The moral was *Academia sucks.*

"At the rate I'm going," Ralph said, "I'm going to be needing that wooden leg myself. I can hardly run around the bases now. They ought to give me the Bill Buckner award."

I'm not going to explain the reference to Bill Buckner. You either know baseball or you don't. In America, baseball and the movies are the mythologies we've got. All the rest is buying and selling.

"There's more to life than running around bases," I told him.

"There's more to life than anything you can name. Licorice, beer, women, horses, poker, whatever you got. Whatever you got, name it. There's more to life than that."

"You're becoming a philosopher in your old age. Anybody who buys a wooden leg has got to be philosophical about it."

Ralph laughed. That was one thing about Ralph I always liked. He laughed a lot. Even when his friends were dumping on him. Or when the gods were kicking his head in. To give you some idea of Ralph's life, take the following into consideration: when his best friend got divorced, he married his friend's wife. And then his wife left him and returned to his friend. And then his ex-wife got pregnant by Ralph, and so she had to leave his friend and return to Ralph. It only hurt when he laughed. And then she finally got fed up and picked up and moved the kids to

Texas. Well, Texas is, as they say, Texas, and the bottom was falling out of the oil business.

When Ralph came up for air, he said, "Shows you what you know. The guy threw in the leg for twenty bucks. He says I can make a couple of hundred from it if I run into the right person."

"Well, the right person will be easy to recognize," I told him.

"What do you mean? Oh, I get it," he said, but this time he didn't laugh. The rain was lashing the windshield and it was getting too hard to see. He turned on the truck's heater. "We have to stop," he said.

I knew he didn't want to. He was in too great a rush to reach his parents before their home was broken into for the third time. Then his old man would surely go berserk and it would be all over.

But I didn't say that. What I said was this: "When you run into the person, really run into him. With any bit of luck you'll sever a leg and make yourself a sure sale."

His knuckles were white. He squinted through the rain, and both of us were exhausted. Mary Jane was doing her stuff because I always get hungry when I smoke. I had a vision of my legs getting up and walking across the highway without me.

"He wanted to give me a break, that's all. We're fellow salesmen. Two pros in the same field," Ralph said.

I thought we should stop and rewrap the leg in plastic. The leg would be of no use to anyone if it got warped. Imagine a killer coming at you with a warped leg. Better a warped leg than a warped sense of humor.

"What's the salesman in the bar being so generous for?"

"I guess he got tired of carrying the stuff around," Ralph said. "I mean, it was just stuff he picked up at a garage sale someplace. It wasn't the stuff he was getting paid to sell."

The book I could understand. *In His Footsteps.* Ralph, after all, was a Bible salesman, but the rest of the mess I couldn't make head nor tail of. "I'd like to meet the salesman someday," I told him. "I want to see if he can sell me the shit he sold you. I suppose you won't get tired of carrying the stuff around?"

"I'm not carrying it around. I just toss it in the trunk. What else do I have back there? Just a lifetime of baby pictures. My kids growing up and turning against me. Why do we have kids anyway?" He turned off the road into a ham and eggs joint. "Besides," he says, "the trouble with you is you think I was buying the stuff. I wasn't buying the stuff. What? You think a Jane Russell poster or a wooden leg is of any interest to me? I need it like I need a hole in the head. I was buying his spiel. I was buying his patter. I was buying his way of life. It's no different than paying for entertainment, and I'd rather be entertained by a salesman who really knows his stuff than spending money on some movie that will end up on TV for free."

"Tell me about it," I told him. I was still sore about taking the secretary to *Peggy Sue Got Married* and not getting laid.

"I just did." We got out into the rain and ran for the ham and eggs. Why do people think that truck drivers have a sixth sense about knowing where to eat? They eat where it's convenient like anybody else. Gourmet food isn't high on their list of priorities. I don't trust truck stops anymore than I trust people from St. Louis.

We took a booth by the window so that Ralph could keep an eye on the truck and its flatbed of treasures. My God, we were bearing great gifts into a world that could safely ignore them. In the back room of the truck stop three or four truckers were standing in line, waiting their turn for a hooker. I didn't say anything. I merely thought about it.

"How do you know?" Ralph asked. He ordered coffee and fried chicken. I stuck with the ham and eggs.

"Because," I told him. "Can't you hear the love moans back there? Or maybe you've reached that stage in life where you can't tell a love moan from a flat tire?"

He nodded. Indeed, he had reached that stage. He frowned and reached for a platter of soggy french fries. Finally he said, "I haven't had a woman in a long time. I just don't feel like going out and telling my life story all over again."

13

"I know what you mean," I told him. "That's why old friends are the best. You don't have to start all over again."

"But I could use a woman."

I inclined my head toward the back room. "I'll treat you," I said.

Ralph shook his head. "No thanks."

"What are you afraid of? Death? Disease? Forget it. It doesn't matter. It's worth the risk. Besides, it's another country and the wench is dead."

He wasn't listening. He got up and brought back a bottle of ketchup from another booth. He drowned the french fries in it. That reminded me of my leg. It hadn't started to bleed again. It hadn't given me a moment's trouble since I had left those gravy lumps behind. Traded intellectual lumps for real ones.

Our waitress was a string-bean without knockers, but I would have taken her into the back room if I could have thought of a way of asking her without starting a fight. I wasn't certain if she was a pure waitress or a waitress-slash-hooker that stray men come across in the depths of latenightmiserystorms. "I ain't never seen it rain like this," she said, putting the platters in front of us. One look at the fried chicken and I knew I had ordered right. It's difficult to do anything bad to an egg. Unless it's a bad egg to begin with.

By the jukebox three women were arguing about unions. "They want Orin to transfer locals, but I told her that if she did that she'd lose all her benefits."

"I thought the benefits transferred."

"No," the black woman said. "I thought so too, but when I came into Local 77 I had to wait seven months for my health card."

"That's too long to wait."

"You're telling me."

"What would happen if your kid got sick?"

"What do you think? They don't care about us. I went down to the local every day for a week and screamed my head off.

They don't listen to me. All they want us to do is turn our tricks and leave them alone."

Outside under the blue-striped awning some children were skipping rope. Their chants filtered into the roadhouse:

> Twelve o'clock striking.
> Mother, may I go out?
> All the boys are waiting,
> For to take me out.
> One will give me an apple,
> One will give me a pear,
> One will give me fifty cents
> To kiss behind the stair.
> I'd rather wash the dishes,
> I'd rather scrub the floor.
> I don't want an apple,
> I don't want a pear,
> I don't want fifty cents
> To kiss behind the stair.

I reiterated my offer to Ralph. He rubbed his forehead with his fingertips. The driving had been an immense strain. Plus he didn't know what was waiting at the other end. His parents might be found murdered by a gang of thugs. "No thanks," he said. "I'm not going to pay for it. I've never had to pay for it, and I don't intend to start now."

I thought about what he told me. "You know what I think? I think I've paid through my teeth for every woman who's slept with me. Not that it's so many, but I don't think there's any end to paying. I'm the King of the Mercy Fucks."

"What's that supposed to mean?" He was building a pyramid out of a stack of napkins by his plate.

"Women feel sorry for you and then they sleep with you. I guess that's what it's supposed to mean."

Ralph shrugged. "Get it any way you can. As long as you don't have to pay for it."

"I'm going to transfer to Miami," the black woman said to her friends. "There are a lot of good jobs in Miami. That's what the man in the union hall said."

"That's where Orin should go, before that boyfriend of hers pistol-whips her again."

"Yeah," the youngest of the three said. She was a pimply red-head whose nervous fingers couldn't stop playing with the buttons on her blouse. She couldn't have been more than fifteen. "But that means you have to live in Miami. The armpit of the world."

"And you'll lose your benefits."

"Well, I'm not going to wait another year to get my health card."

"Do you ever think about your ex-wife sleeping with other men?" Ralph asked me.

"Not much. Why?"

"Because I think about it all the time."

A Greek man in an apron, maybe the owner of the place, worked the cash register. He wore a baseball cap that said GREG'S HARDWARE, and as he rang up the hamburgers and whores and cokes and fries and plovers' eggs and caviar and newspapers and missionary positions and telephone numbers and waterglasses and toothpicks, he sang:

> There lived an old lord by the Northern Sea,
> > Bow'e down!
> There lived an old lord by the Northern Sea,
> > Bow and balance to me!
> There lived an old lord by the Northern Sea,
> > I'll be true to my love,
> > If my love'll be true to me.

The world was drowning in things it had no business thinking about.

"And I can't stand it," Ralph added. "I think about it all the time and it makes me sick." He started to cry. Right then and there. The strain of the rain, the driving, his parents getting robbed, his wife taking the kids to Texas, it was getting to him, neat and quick. I didn't want to embarrass him, so I got up and went over to the jukebox to find something to play. The three whores parted slightly to let me through.

"Nothin' on that," the black woman said.

"Play E-3."

"If you want to put your finger on something, don't waste it on that button."

I studied the list, each song coded, given a letter and a number. The Azmak Mounds of Southern Bulgaria. Air Reconnaissance. The Origins of Microwave Love. The Finglesham Man. Body Montage. Ethno-Botany of the Willing Virgin. American Agriculture. Big Bucks. Killer Lust. Passport to Passion. Concordance to the Poems of Ralph Waldo Emerson. Tertiary Gastropods. The Consumers Guide to Human Flesh. King Lear. World War III. Stoned Wheat Thins. I Left My Heart in Gebel-el-Akhden. Ebb Tide. Le Crime Etait Presque Parfait.

"Find anything you like, honey?"

I dropped two quarters in and played Nat King Cole. He made me think of my high school days.

I waited for Ralph to pull himself together and then brought him a newspaper. I thought we could play a couple of ponies to keep our minds off things. Of course it had occurred to me that if the whores needed a ride to Miami then maybe we could accommodate them. Then maybe they could accommodate us.

The paper said:

FRESH EVIDENCE SHOWS ANCIENT ROMANS' LUST

Pompeii, Italy. (AP) Archaeologists have made new X-rated discoveries in Pompeii, unearthing fresh evidence of the libertine habits of the ancient Romans.

Pornographic mosaics depicting combinations of two, three or four men and women were found in what experts describe as a combination bathhouse and bordello.

I took the paper back. Ralph had enough on his mind without being reminded of the Golden Age.

"Sorry," he said.

"Forget it." Mabel, set the table. Don't forget the salt, vinegar, mustard, pepper. The blonde waitress without tits crossed to our booth and started to clear off a few platters. There were still pieces of fried chicken left. She might have asked if we were done, but she didn't. She could have said whatsthematteryoudontlikethecooking but maybe she took that for granted. What she said was: "If you guys want your fortunes told, Madame Zorina's in the back room."

"What's she do? Read peckers?"

She tossed me a look to kill and humped the platters away, walking like a Long Island girl, throwing her groin out. I asked her for a refill, then caught myself wondering how many hours of my life have been spent ordering food and staring into the sacred fountains of black coffee. Probably whole days of my life have been spent unwrapping sugar cubes or tearing open tiny white packets that have been painted with pictures of songbirds. Mockingbirds mostly.

"What's the good of a union card," the fifteen-year-old asked, "if everybody's going around shooting at everybody?" But what she was talking about I didn't know. I had lost track.

"I know a woman who used to come here all the time," said the brunette who had the word LOVE tattooed on her left forearm. She was the best-looking of the three. "She poisoned her own baby. Poured rat poison down its mouth. The kid was not more than eight months old. No bigger than a rat herself."

"Maybe that's why she did it," said the fifteen-year-old uneasily.

"What do you mean?"

"I mean the kid being so scrawny and all."

The black woman gave her a funny look. Under the awning the girls chanted, "Mama doll, mama doll, go upstairs, Mama doll, mama doll, comb your hairs."

"She thought it was the end of the world," the tattooed whore said. "She didn't want her child to live to see the end of the world."

"And so she ended it for him."

"Rat poison," the black woman said with disgust, moving aside to allow a woman in a wheelchair to slide by. It had to be Madame Zorina, a seventy-year-old white-haired woman dressed like a gypsy, with her blue skirt hiked up to her waist. I told Ralph, "Here's your big chance." He didn't understand. He kept his head down, staring at the carvings. JESUS SAVES.

Madame Zorina was wheeling her red plastic dangling earrings towards us. Whenever any person has any part of her body missing, a man'll notice it right off. Women too. People are like that. We notice what's missing before we notice what's there. Madame Zorina's left leg had been amputated. "Go get your leg," I told Ralph, "and maybe we can strike a deal."

"Sure."

"It's better than sitting here and crying into your beer. Besides, you know you should get rid of that thing."

Ralph shook his head, but then he gave in and went outside. I watched him. He was right. He was walking like an old man. Maybe the wooden leg would turn out to be a good investment.

"I have something here you can use," I told Madame Zorina. She stopped at the edge of our booth and adjusted an earring. "Keep it in your pants."

"I'm not talking about that," I told her.

"How refreshing. Everybody else does," she said. Her face was so round I thought I could draw a perfect circle around it. But it would be no halo.

"I'm talking about a wooden leg. You need a wooden leg, don't you?"

I must have touched a nerve, for she immediately pulled her skirt down and rolled her head from side to side, licking her mouth with her tongue. "Suffer me to abide this single day," she called out to no one in particular, but reaching to the farther reaches of the hashery, "and devise some plan for the manner of my exile and means of living for my children, since their father cares not to provide for his babes therewith. Then pity

19

them; thou too hast children of thine own; thou needs must have a kindly heart. For my own lot I care naught, though I am an exile. But for those babes I weep, that they should learn what sorrow means."

By the time she reached the last few lines, she was staring straight into my eyes searching for a soul that I knew was not there. The three whores by the jukebox pointed to their heads and made circles with their forefingers, their way of warning me that the woman was not all there, mentally, I mean. The physical parts I have already mentioned.

By the time Ralph reached the awning with his treasures, the jump-rope girls had left, and when he came inside everybody in the place turned to look. Indeed he appeared quite ludicrous with his head glazed with rain. A man can lose a lot of hair in twenty-five years. He carried the leg to our booth and rolled it under Madame Zorina's nose. Unfortunately, she was off and running. "On all sides sorrow pens me in. Who shall say this is not true? But all is not lost."

Ralph, sensing another lost cause, didn't even bother to sit down. He hovered over the leg as if it were a pearl of great price. I, however, did not feel like letting Medea off the hook. The Greek at the cash register sang:

> My father keeps a public house
> On yonder river side.
> Go ye, go there, and enter in,
> And this night abide.

The mention of money brings any actress back to earth, and so I said, "I guess you can't afford it, right? That's what you're trying to tell us, even if my friend and I offer you the deal of the century?"

Medea, cum Madame Zorina, fished around in her ample blouse and plucked out a purple change purse tied to a white string. "I can afford anything I want," she said, "but it doesn't look like my leg."

"It's not supposed to look like your leg," I told her. "If it looked like an exact duplicate of your leg, you couldn't afford it. It would cost you ten, fifteen thousand dollars."

She leaned over the top of the table and sniffed at the knee. She ran her hand down the leg, stopped at the foot, and carefully examined the toe. "I had a beautiful foot," she said.

"I don't doubt it."

"Don't fool around with me. I can buy you bums three times over."

Ralph laughed. He knew well the advantages of laughing at the jokes of a potential customer. "That's no big deal. Anybody in this place can do that."

"But nobody can give you a wooden leg worth ten thousand dollars for less than five hundred." I looked at Ralph to make certain that I hadn't dropped too far too fast. Icarus in the lake of high finance.

"Five hundred?"

"Can't beat it."

She studied the outside of her purse, but she didn't open it. "I can make the rain stop."

"What's that to me?"

"Give me the leg or I'll make it rain forever. Everything on the earth will drown."

"Give me a break, lady."

"Madame Zorina to you."

Ralph picked up the leg. "I guess I'll put it back," he said. "I can get a couple of thousand dollars for it from a hospital."

"When the Thunderbird flaps his great wings," she said, "he makes thunder, and then the great winds come, so loud you cannot hear the beating of your own heart."

"How about two hundred dollars?" I asked. "I mean that's nothing. That's practically giving it away."

The door opened and the jump-rope girls dashed in. "Come quick, Momma," one of them called to the black woman standing by the jukebox, hovering with her great wings over Nat

21

King Cole and the Waterbaby Song. The jump-rope girl herself was a waterbaby born of incest, and finally would end up in heaven. "That man is back again and he's beating up Orin. He's beating her up with his fists."

"Where?"

"In back, by the river."

And we all went running, except for Madame Zorina who stayed put, stroking her change purse and repeating her babble.

"I'll think it over," she said, but it was too late. One minute she was one person, and the next minute she was another. It's impossible, the textbooks say, to do business with a person like that. I should have known better. Ralph and I together should have known we were wasting our time. Damn that salesman from St. Louis, I thought.

"Alas! This is not the first time you have done me mischief, Creon. Nor is it the first time you have stained my reputation and caused me mischief. Whoever is wise will not make his children too clever, for besides the reputation they get for idleness, they receive only hatred from the other citizens." She inhabited a country that no longer existed, and Ralph and I had to reach it with all due speed.

As we crossed behind the truck stop and saw the river all swollen and flush, zipping along, I asked Ralph, "What are you going to do with that thing?"

"I don't know. I didn't trust her to leave it there," he said. Behind us the whores and the jump-rope girls were shouting Orin's name, and out of a back door the Greek cashier emerged, swinging a meat cleaver. At least he was no longer singing those awful songs so that was something to be thankful for. But the river wasn't getting any smaller or any slower, what with the rain beating its head in. And chill. Chilled to the bone.

"There she is," the fifteen-year-old shouted, pointing. Two of the other whores were trying to hold the youngsters back. The black man who had been pummeling Orin pushed her away, violently shoving her down the river bank, into the water, where she grew larger and larger and seemed to sweep by us.

Four or five truckers took off after the man. I sure didn't want to be in his shoes when they caught him.

Ralph zig-zagged a hundred yards or so downstream, skidded down the steep and muddy bank that was dotted with broken beer bottles and prophylactics, and held forth the wooden leg to the drowning whore. I had a feeling it was going to prove useful for something. "Grab it!" he shouted to the woman who wore her hair cropped short like a boy and whose thin black dress was torn, but now that her head was back in the water and her mouth was open to the current and the rain, she didn't understand or she didn't hear or she was in a panic fighting the water and the brutal beating. She made no effort to reach out for the foot or the ankle or the thigh. A wonder of modern craftsmanship.

"She's blind," the brunette shouted.

"What?" I asked.

"Don't you understand anything?" the waitress asked. "Orin's been blind since birth. She's never been in the river before. I bet she doesn't even know where she is." But even as the waitress spoke and pointed, Orin had turned herself face downward, placed her knees and hands upon the rocky bottom, and now was trying to crawl to shore, moving slowly like a baby or a wounded animal or something that had poison poured down her throat. Ralph released the leg and waded in after her, trying to reach the woman before she swallowed all the river, but Orin, who was only a little speck, not more than five foot four and who probably weighed only slightly more than a hundred pounds sopping wet, reached out with her right arm to push Ralph away, not knowing who he was, and then suddenly, "Sonuvabitch, sonuvabitch, sonabitch," changed her mind and grabbed him by the shirt and tried to drag him down on top of her.

"Stand up!" I shouted to her. "Stand up! It's not that deep." But the others were running down the bank too, so I ran in. Now there were two on one, and I grabbed her waist from behind, my hands feeling the elastic of her panties, and tried to

23

pull her upright, and she was screaming "Help! Help! Help!" and then howling, bleeding from her mouth where her friend had beaten her, and bleeding from her arms where the rocks had cut her, then crying out to God or Jesus or to somebody whose name I didn't know, and fighting nasty and dirty all the time, trying to pull free from us, as I grabbed her and lifted her from the water, trying not to lose my own footing, and then the Greek helping, and all Ralph and I could say was, "It's all right, it's all right, it's all right," and finally, while some giant fish swallowed the wooden leg, we dragged her onto the bank and the three of us lay there, with the Greek standing over us, his apron dripping, and Orin sobbing, then howling, her stockings in shreds, and her shoes long gone, and I finally realized that this was not the way I wanted to spend my life, and the three whores surrounded us and gently placed an oil tablecloth around her and picked her up, and they all walked up the bank with the Greek following them muttering, and the jump-rope girls singing:

> Marry in green,
> Ashamed to be seen,
>
> Marry in brown,
> Move to town,
>
> Marry in blue,
> Always be true,
>
> Marry in yellow,
> Ashamed of your feller.

They didn't, trailing into the truck stop, finish it, though the ending was clear: Marry in black, very bad luck.

Ralph and I lay on our backs and swallowed water. Amazing how quickly we had been left alone except for one of the jump-rope girls standing up on the bank looking down upon us, spying. As if we had done nothing, and maybe we had. If we had been in Florida, as we had planned, and if the sun were shining, and if it were a hot and humid day, we would have stripped and plunged into the water ourselves, swimming and absolving, but it really was not that warm. Also, how rare it is to see our friends naked. Or even ourselves.

"If we don't get out of these clothes," I said, "we're going to die of pneumonia."

"I know."

But we didn't move. The rain was letting up, so we just lay there, mud-soaked. "Did you ever see *Peggy Sue Got Married?*" I asked him.

"No. Did you?" He wasn't laughing. And his face was scratched. Good thing his wife had left him or he would have had a hard time explaining that one. Yes, dear, I pulled a blind whore out of a river.

"Yeah." We were both breathing pretty heavy, but Ralph, because of his softball games, was in much better shape. His stomach was flat. Mine was kind of a small mountain waiting for Lilliputians and their chariots. "Yeah," I repeated. It was getting darker and harder to see the river.

"Like it?"

I shook my head. "Actually, I don't know. I'm losing my critical perspective. I don't know what to think about anything. Except we're going to die. That's all I know, and you can't build a holy mound of bones out of that."

After a while Ralph asked, "Did you pay the check?"

"No. Did you?"

"We ran out of there like a bat out of hell."

"Well, we probably don't have to anyway. Right?"

I shrugged. Some people make you pay for everything. Besides we might not have done the Greek any favors. In the distance there was a sound of a gun being fired, or a truck backfiring. It could have been one or the other. "What time is it?" Ralph asked. "I promised to call my parents before six to find out if they've been broken into again."

I looked at my wrist and showed it to Ralph. "You want to wade in and look for it?" he asked.

25

"No. It's not worth anything," I told him, finally standing up and breathing in the winter air. "You can buy a watch on the street for three or four bucks nowadays. I just want to get changed before I get my death of cold and get transported to a country where women don't wear any underwear and you can get a decent meal for less than a dollar."

I helped Ralph to his feet and we started up the river bank and toward the parking lot. The girl holding her jump-rope didn't follow us. She merely kept her eyes straight ahead, gazing at something I could no longer see. The Most Athletic had gone to Vietnam and lost an eye. The Most Intellectual had experimented with LSD and had hurled himself out a hotel window in Boston. The Most Friendly had divorced three times over. The Most Romantic had never married. The Funniest was lost; the Most Curious was damned.

The gypsy actress saw us through the plate-glass window and wheeled out to greet us. In her hands were five crisp hundred-dollar bills. "I thought about your offer," she said. "I've changed my mind. It's a bargain. Here's your money."

Ralph shook his head. "You can have it for free," he told her, "if you can find it. It's down in the river somewhere."

"What do you mean?"

"I mean it's down in the river. Now if you'll excuse me, I've got to go to the men's room."

"You idiot. I wanted that leg." By now the rain had stopped completely. Maybe she had kept her part of the bargain. Under the windshield wiper of the Dodge was a folded piece of paper. While Ralph got out fresh clothes, I read it:

AND ALL THINGS, WHATSOEVER WE SHALL ASK IN PRAYER, BELIEVING WE SHALL RECEIVE. (Matt. 21–22)

This quote has been sent to you for good luck, the original copy is from the Netherlands. It has been around the world 5 times. The luck has been brought to you. You will receive good luck within 4 days on receiving this letter providing you in turn sent it back out. This is no joke. You will receive it in the mail. Send copies of this letter to people you want to receive good luck. Do not send money, for fate has no price on it. Do not keep this letter, it must leave your hands 96 hours after you receive it. A police officer received $70,000.00. Joe Elliot received $450,000 and lost it because he broke the chain. While in the Philippines General Weles lost his life 3 days after he received the chain letter. He failed to circulate the quote. However, before his death, he received $775,000. Please send 20 copies and see what happens to you on the 4th day. This comes from Venezuela and was written by Saul Anthony DeCaccio, a missionary from South America. I myself forwarded it to you. Since the chain makes a tour of the world, you must make 20 identical copies of this one. Send it to your friends, parents, and associates. After a few days, you will get a surprise. This is true if you aren't suprstitious. Take note of the following. Constantino Dias received the chain in 1953. He asked his secretary to make 20 copies and sent them out. A few days later he won the lottery for $20,000 in his country. Carlo Dedio, an office employee, received the chain and forgot it; a few days later he lost his job. He found the letter and sent it to 20 people. Five days later, he found an even better job. De Bantonchild received the chain, not believing it, threw it away and 9 days later he died. For no known reason whatsoever should this chain be broken.

REMINDER: Send no money. Please do not ignore it. It works.

"What is it?" Ralph asked, handing me a clean shirt and a pair of pants.

"It's our reward, I guess. Our reward." I folded the paper and handed it to him. Zorina was on her way to the river.

"Well, at least I'm not going home empty-handed," Ralph said, without opening the letter, without reading it. "I hate to go home empty-handed."

"Tell me about it," I said, watching the lights come on and inhaling the smell of diesel.

"I just did," he said. "I just did." While he limped to the phone booth to make his call, I climbed into the Dodge to retrieve our high school yearbook. We were just another class like any other.

easter
sunday

My mother and I had moved, right in
the height or depths of the Depres-
sion, over to New Mexico, in a town
near Carlsbad, where her friend Milly
Stamps lived. I was eleven years old,
Mom was in her forties, and Dad was
dead. I had taken to dreaming about
him, but the dreams were always about
him, never *with* him if you know what
I mean. For example, sometime between Good Friday and Easter Sunday,
I had the same dream twice. I was
walking home from school and I was
wearing, not my own clothes, but a
jacket and shirt belonging to my old

man. The walk was a long one, much longer than my usual three-mile hike. To take a short cut, I ended up in someone's backyard in a lawn surrounded by a chain link fence. I could get in, but I couldn't get out. And three large German shepherd dogs came barking at me. I called for help and a boy my age came out the backdoor of a neighboring house. He wasn't concerned for me. He was only wondering why I was trespassing. And then I woke up.

Every time I wore a hat or a coat belonging to my old man I got into trouble. It was as simple as that. On Sunday morning, I told my mother the dream. She couldn't make head nor tails of it either. I never knew exactly what she thought about my father—I knew he beat her up once or twice, but didn't mean nothing by it—and I never asked her. I never could find the right time. That morning we sat at the kitchen table while she read aloud from her Bible. It was too far to go to church.

> *And when he had called unto him his twelve disciples, he gave them power against unclean spirits to cast them out, and to heal all manner of sickness and all manner of disease.*
>
> *Now the names of the twelve apostles are these: The first, Simon, who is called Peter, and Andrew his brother; James the son of Zebedee, and John his brother.*

Etc. It was a long one. "And whosoever shall give to drink unto one of those little ones a cup of cold water only in the name of a disciple, verily I say unto you, he shall in no wise lose his reward," she concluded. She looked up from the book. "Don't make a face," she said, "just put on your jacket. We've been invited to Milly's for Easter Supper." I put on my father's jacket—the only thing he actually left me—and off we walked, four or five miles to Milly's. Momma smoked the whole way.

My mother didn't weigh much, but she was the hardest worker I knew, and the strongest walker (we owned a motorcycle, but she wouldn't ride it on Sunday), a thin woman with long black hair that hung down in a braid. Her skin was dark brown from the sun, and so was mine. Skin like leather, I guess, the kind that invites all kinds of cancers later. She said we were tough, and maybe we were. Neither of us wore shoes. We carried them, so they wouldn't be covered with dust. We didn't talk much, except about ice cream. Milly had promised to make some ice cream. Strawberry I hoped. Strawberry was my favorite then. Nowadays I wouldn't eat it if you paid me. But that just goes to show you how Time changes things.

Since Milly had invited us to dinner, Momma felt obliged to bring her something. We weren't in any position to bring her food or wine, and although the wildflower solution was perfectly acceptable, Milly had flowers of her own, and so Momma brought her a copy of a book she had swiped from a drugstore somewhere, swiped because she would have been too embarrassed to show the title to the check-out clerk: *Naked on Roller Skates* by Maxwell Bodenheim. I guess nobody reads Bodenheim today, but in the early thirties, he was all the rage. Not that Momma would have cared or known, because she wasn't by a long shot the world's best reader. She loved *True Detective* and a few movie magazines and the Bible and a book about Jesus, and then whatever she could find. *Naked on Roller Skates* was just one of those books she had found. The fact that she found it on the rental bookshelf in the back of a drugstore didn't necessarily mean she didn't find it.

Outside Milly's tiny house we put on our shoes, and when we went inside there were a bunch of people I had never seen before and would never see again. At least not in real life. And there were no other children around either, which meant that the afternoon was not going to be much fun, especially with all the emphasis on Jesus rising from the dead and sitting on the right hand of God and the world trembling and skies thundering. No matter how you cut it, Easter is not Christmas. At least on Christmas, a boy can look forward to getting presents, even if the presents are practical things like secondhand shoes and not something that he would ask for if he had dared to ask:

Railroad trains, and wind-up cars, and a baseball glove, and and and . . .

And Momma, not being comfortable around strangers, sat on one end of the couch with her Bible on her lap, and I sat next to her reading it with her. It was that kind of an Easter Sunday. People sat about Mrs. Stamps's house, doing pretty much as they pleased, with nobody bothering nobody else. Mrs. Stamps had accepted my mother's awkward gift with a great deal of gush, but I could tell from her embarrassment that she, no matter how long she lived, had no intention of reading it.

Another woman came in. She couldn't have weighed more than a hundred pounds and her hair was taffy-colored. Mrs. Stamps introduced us all around. She said her name was Bonnie. Bonnie Thornton, and she was something of a poet. When she was fifteen, she said, she had married a boy named Roy Thornton. But she told her aunt that she wasn't using the name Thornton anymore. That so, said Mrs. Stamps. That's so, said Bonnie. She took the book from Mrs. Stamps and opened it. She read it aloud:

> Listen, Terry—any man can beat up a girl's body. That's no trick. I want an A number one, guaranteed bastard. I want him to beat my heart and beat my brain. I want him to hurt me so I'll bet wise. I want him to lug me everywhere. All the lowest dives, the phoniest ginmills . . . I want him to throw me up against everybody—the crummiest wood-chucks . . . the worst fourflushers . . . everybody. I want to meet the coldest women—the women who get their diamonds and cars and then start to bawl about how sad and unlucky they've been . . . I want to run into everybody just once . . . They say a girl can't do it. They say she runs into a smashup every time. Well, believe me, she'll smash up in a village cupboard too, if she can't hide herself and settle down. That's a lot of newspaper hokum . . .

Mrs. Thornton, or whatever her last name was, had a voice like honey, soft and sweet. I took a liking to her right away.

"So that's your son, Mrs. Wylie?" she asked, closing the book and tossing it casually to one side, a dismissal that I noticed brought my mother no end of hurt.

Momma nodded. "He's my son, the man around the house since his father died. Peter, shake hands with Mrs. Thornton."

"Parker," Mrs. Thornton said. "Bonnie Parker." I took her hand and her grip was strong. My father had taught me to shake hands. "Look a person straight in the eye and don't be limp about it. Strong grip."

"Only son?"

"Yes, Ma'am," Momma said, with the Bible still opened on her lap. "He had a brother Andrew, but he died of the chicken pox."

"Do children still die of the chicken pox?" Miss Parker asked.

"I guess some do," my momma said without flinching.

"And what grade are you in?"

"Fifth grade," I answered. She still held my hand. From the outside two men came in carrying some ice for the ice cream bucket. One of the men, the shorter of the two, leaned a shotgun near the door.

"I don't want no guns in the house," Mrs. Stamps said. Like my mother, she too was a widow, and had no man to protect her.

"It's just a hunting rifle," one of the men said. "In case we decide to do some hunting later." They carried the block of ice into the kitchen.

"He's the fifth grade spelling champ," Momma said.

"I'm a spelling champ too," Miss Parker said. "Maybe we should have a spelling bee sometime."

"I'd like to," I said. And I would have too. I would have liked the opportunity to prove myself to those people, though of course I had no idea why. Maybe because they were outsiders and new. Anything new in those days was worth paying attention to.

Mrs. Stamps crossed to the door. She was going to move the shotgun outside her house, but Miss Parker stopped her. "Leave it alone, Aunt Milly. Don't you be fussing with what don't concern you. After all it belongs to Ray and he doesn't want nobody messing with it."

Mrs. Stamps leaned the shotgun against the wall where it belonged and sighed. "It is Sunday," she said. "And Easter at that. Our Lord rose from the dead to save us from our sins."

"We all know that, Aunt Milly," Miss Parker said. "Everybody knows that. Don't we, Peter."

"Yes, Ma'am."

"It's right here in the Bible," Momma said. And she started to read again:

And it was about the sixth hour, and there was darkness all over the earth until the ninth hour. And the sun was darkened, and the veil of the temple was rent in the midst.

And when Jesus had cried with a loud voice, he said, Father, into thy hands I commend my spirit: and having said thus, he gave up the ghost.

Miss Parker nodded. Finally she said, "I write poetry myself you know. Do you want to hear some?"

Mrs. Stamps sat down in a chair and wiped her hands on her apron. "Even when Bonnie was a little girl she used to love to make up songs and sing. Used to sing all the time. Used to make up the cleverest songs."

Bonnie walked behind the table and raised her arms as if she were conducting an orchestra. She started to recite, but the men didn't even come out from the kitchen. I could hear their voices, but I couldn't make out what they were talking about.

> "We don't think we're too tough or desperate.
> We know the law always wins.
> We've been shot at before
> And we do not ignore
> That death is the wages of sin."

Miss Parker no sooner finished one poem when she would launch into another. I reckoned she must have written hundreds of them, and I could have sat through them all.

34

> "They call them cold-blooded killers:
> They say they are heathen and mean,
> But I say this with pride,
> That I once knew Clyde
> When he was honest and upright and clean."

And on and on she went. I could tell that Momma didn't think much of it at all, but then she had been raised on finer poetry—Wordsworth and the Bible and things like that.

I liked it though. As I said, she had a real sweet voice. I would have given anything to hear her sing.

Near the end of the reading, the four men came in from the kitchen. They were carrying bottles of beer and had been drinking. Mrs. Stamps was clearly flustered, but she introduced the men all around: Clyde Barrow, Joe Palmer, Raymond Hamilton, and Henry Methvin.

Momma shook hands and mumbled please to meet you, but I knew she didn't mean it. Me, I liked the men right away. While Miss Parker went on reciting, the man named Clyde bent down and showed me his tattoo. On his right forearm there were the letters USN.

"Were you in the navy, Mr. Barrow?"

He shook his head. "Call me Clyde, Ma'am. Everybody calls me Clyde." He might as well have asked my mother to walk on water. No way was she going to do that.

> "From heartbreak some people have suffered,
> From weariness some people have died.
> But take it all in all,
> Your troubles are small,
> Till you get like Bonnie and Clyde,"

said Miss Parker. None of the men were paying too much attention. Mrs. Stamps excused herself and retreated to the kitchen.

"Bonnie, did you tell the boy about the time we tried to rob a bank and there was nobody there?" The man named Clyde let out with a guffaw and slapped his knee. The other men, looking out the window, chuckled.

"You sonuvabitch," Miss Parker shouted. "I'm reciting my poetry. You have no right to barge in here and interrupt."

Mr. Barrow hung his head, a real hangdog expression on his face.

"Sorry," he said. Then to me, "You come around and see me sometime and I'll tell you all about it." He squeezed my shoulders and winked. "How we go running into this here bank, shouting and screaming all get out, and there's just one old guy there and he starts to laugh."

"Goddamn you!" Miss Parker shouted.

Momma turned red. "Go get your jacket, Peter. I think we're going to have to go."

"You can't go, Ma'am," the man named Raymond said. "We ain't even had supper yet."

"I'm not feeling so good," Momma lied. "It's my stomach. I get upsets in the stomachs all the time." She closed her Bible and stood up.

"Someday they'll go down together," Miss Parker recited quite loudly, dipping a crystal cup into the punch bowl. "And they'll bury them side by side. To few it'll be grief, To the law a relief, But it's death for Bonnie and Clyde."

"And for a moment I thought the old man was laughing at me, and just as Ray here was getting ready to plug him one, he turns to us and says 'Ain't no money in it.'" Mr. Barrow just kept talking right over Miss Parker's poetry and she was getting fit to be tied.

"What do you mean there's no money here. This is a bank, ain't it. If there ain't no money in a bank where in hell is there goin' to be any money?"

Momma picked up my father's jacket and her own, grabbed me by the shoulders to propel me toward the kitchen. "I'm sorry, you all," Momma told them. "I just don't feel well at all. I'm going to have to go home and get some rest."

"You get better, Mrs. Wylie," Miss Parker said, sitting down in the space vacated by Momma. She finished the punch in one gulp.

36

"'Bank's been closed four days now,' that old geezer said," Mr. Barrow called after me as Momma pushed me into the kitchen.

"God I'll never forget that one," he added.

"Clyde, there's a car coming this way," one of the men called.

In the kitchen, Mrs. Stamps was standing at the sink. She wasn't doing anything, not fussing over her Easter Dinner at all. She was just standing at the sink, staring out at the sun over the mountains. The sun was a long long way off. Even I could see she was trembling.

"Momma, who are those people," I asked, as she helped me on with my father's jacket. "And what was the man talking about robbing banks for?"

"Shhh!" Momma said. "He was just telling stories. You know how men get when they drink. They just start making up stories."

"You mean like Bible stories?"

"The Bible ain't no story," she said. "Milly, I think you've got more guests coming."

"I didn't invite nobody," she said, turning around finally, wiping her hands on her apron. The sun through the kitchen window caught her diamond ring just right.

The men in the living room had become quiet all of a sudden. And Miss Parker too. I tried to remember some of the poetry but I couldn't. My head was swimming with too many things.

"What are you doing, Dorothy?" Mrs. Stamps asked my mother. "You can't be going, can you? You haven't had any supper."

"I'm sorry, Milly, but my stomach is upset something powerful. We really have to go. I'm sorry. I am really very sorry." Momma's face held the same hangdog expression that Mr. Barrow's had.

Milly didn't say anything. She merely put her hand on Momma's right shoulder. I thought it was a strange gesture for women, but Mrs. Stamps looked as if she were going to burst into tears.

"The boy and I'll come back later in the week," Momma told her.

"Let me send over some food for you later. I'll get my niece and her friend to drive some supper over to you."

"Don't go to all that trouble."

"No trouble."

"My stomachs are too upset. I couldn't eat a thing."

"But it's Easter Sunday, and there's the boy . . ."

"Aunt Milly, did you invite the Sheriff up to supper?" Bonnie was standing in the kitchen entranceway. One hand was on her hip. The other hand pressed against the archway. The sun caught her red hair like a flame.

"I didn't invite nobody but Dorothy and her boy," she told her.

"Well, he and his deputy are out in the front yard now, nosing around our car."

"I know him. I'll go out."

"No, ask them in, Aunt Milly. Ask them in for dinner. We got plenty to go around, haven't we?"

I could smell the ham filling the kitchen. And then it hit me full force just how much I missed my dad. And Andrew. And all of us sitting down to dinner together. Which was what Easter was I guess. Momma rushed me to the back door and out into the yard. Milly's three German shepherds started barking. This time, however, Momma didn't stop to take off her shoes. She walked so fast across the dusty fields that we were almost running.

"Are your stomachs hurting real bad, Momma?"

She didn't answer. She just kept walking. The afternoon sun didn't move. And then there was a shot. A rifle shot from the house.

"Momma, did you hear that?"

She shook her head.

"I want to go back and see!"

Momma grabbed me by the arm. "No, no, Peter," she said. "Just get down. Get down." She kneeled down in the dust and pulled me down too. We listened, but there were three more shots and some cars being started. The sounds of the rifles and the cars carried in the air so clear, they didn't seem far away at all. Everything was very close. Milly's dogs were barking something fierce.

At the sound of the shots, Momma crossed herself and started to pray: "Our Father Who art in heaven, Hallowed be thy name . . ."

I couldn't think of anything else to do so I started to pray with her. After all it must be very lonely to be praying all by yourself in the presence of someone else. I started to pray thinking that me and my father shared the same idea. With all the fuss going on about us, we didn't want my momma to be lonely.

merité
des
femmes

New York. New York. Two in the morning at Kennedy Airport. A rainy morning. I had been sitting in Pittsburgh for nearly four hours and I merely—merely!—wanted to get home. The woman in front of me, about the same age as I, dressed in a beige suit, like myself, and carrying, like myself, one suitcase and one briefcase, and one book, a French one, I believe, suggested we share a cab to Manhattan, and so we did. We lived roughly—roughly!—in the same part of town.

It had been a long trip from the coast, and, at first, I thought I would not talk. Just listen, I thought. Two tired women just wanting to get home. Not that I had anyone waiting for me. My ten-year-old daughter and her younger brother were staying with their father in Brooklyn Heights. Even so. One's tiny apartment is always better than any hotel. I had been raised by strict Methodist parents. Thus, it was never my fate to feel comfortable, alone—alone!—in a strange hotel. Something illicit is suggested. Something illicit vaguely missed. Like an affair with a married man that goes on and on and on. Hopeless to the end. And something vaguely missed. Like turning to him at three in the morning. Or having breakfast with him on Sundays. The sleeve-but-not-the-arm syndrome. No clothes in the closet.

My co-rider was Simone Morrill. I had heard the name, of course. For two reasons. I had read her biography of Nathalia Crane. All 438 pages of it. Critical overkill, I thought, considering the lack of fame of its subject.

Miss Crane, it seems, in the mid-1920s, had published a book of poetry. The poetry has been well received by numerous critics and fellow writers. Nothing especially remarkable about that, except Ms. Crane had been all of ten years old at the time of her debut. A child prodigy might well be expected in chess or music or mathematics. But never in poetry. Never? Rarely. How can one make poetry when one has lived so little, has experienced so little? That was the question Ms.—Ms.!—Morrill had explored at length. Her answer: In spite of everything, one makes poetry out of words. I didn't doubt it, but I did. A contradiction, I suppose:

> Oh, when a gleaming motor glides
> From out a dusky haze,
> Bethink you of the flowers there
> Within a tonneau vase.

Bethink! even. Then what happens to child prodigies who happen to make their mark in writing? Being a child prodigy, however, was far beyond my ambitions and state of being. Like

41

my newfound companion, I was in my early fifties, a first-time mother late in life, but too old to be a prodigy about anything else, though I suppose as a young girl I too had tried my hand at verses. I had not produced anything of the quality of Miss Crane, although I felt the prodigy had been overly influenced by Emily Dickinson. Of course, one might be impressed by any young child who places a tonneau vase within her poem. William Benét had been. So too Nunnally Johnson. Impressing readers is one thing. Impressing Time is another.

And then I knew of my companion because, shades of the small world, Ms. Morrill's daughter—Laura—had once taught at the Paine School of Girls where I was presently employed. A private school for girls. Rich girls. Girls who could fly, in their Gucci hairdos, to Paris for spring break, while my nine-year-old son and I debated the wisdom of parting with seven dollars a ticket to watch men dressed up like turtles subdue the universe, a universe that had been emptied of everything but pizzas. Or while my daughter and I dragged the dirty laundry into school, to sneak it in with the costumes needing washing by the dramatics society. A nickel here. A quarter there. Upstairs in any unused nook and cranny of the school, Laura held personal conference after conference, ostensibly tutoring English and Latin, while all the while taking each lost student under her wing, prying every scandal, self-doubt, ambition, hurt, or wound into the blaze of psychoanalysis, of which Laura was a prime mover. In her prime, Laura was the eccentric teacher extraordinaire. Students begged their way into Laura's courses. I frequently overheard her telling jokes in the hallway, while I myself holed up in the school's development office. And a hole it was too. My goal was to raise money, not diphthongs. At least that was one of my goals. I had other goals, personal goals, as well. My husband had left me with the children while he had driven to California to make it big in the movies. I would never forgive him for that. The cab paused for a light. A black man urinating through a chain link fence shouted for everyone to hear, "Step up and see the Greatest Show on Earth!" Fine, I thought. Welcome home.

Some things you couldn't forgive strangers for either. Though as I had turned the corner on fifty, I was beginning to realize that even those who had been closest to me, had been central to my life, were becoming stranger and stranger.

"The city's getting less liveable, every year," Simone observed. She had insisted upon first names. "Every year." I could not help but agree. "One's life gets more unliveable each and every year," I thought she said, but perhaps I myself had thought it and brought unspoken thoughts into being. But she and I were very different. The lines on her face bespoke despair. Hers was a long face, not particularly good-looking, with a wide mouth smeared ungainly with lipstick, and large teeth that clipped and bit the words, words thought through and framed and richly accented. Blue eyes that missed very little. Her hair, brown and gray, was pinned in a tight bun at the top of her head.

"I don't know why I keep going out on these lectures," she added. "Traveling's too exhausting and New York too traumatic to return to. But when your only child dies, one can either mope around the house or throw one's self into one's work. I refuse to be a moper. Laura would want me out there, carrying on the work."

I nodded. "We all miss her." And we did. Laura had contracted—contracted!—cancer, had given up a breast, underwent session after session of chemotherapy, had to quit teaching, moved to London with Arkin, her husband, who had been part of a major brokerage house, and then, in the final, horrible months, was tended around the clock with private nurses. Nice that her husband's money could buy her that little bit of comfort, I suppose. When she had been well, and spilling over with gossip, and not cells, I had envied her money, her New York apartment with its roof garden, her coterie of famous friends.

After her illness, of course, I envied her nothing.

When Laura, recovering from her mastectomy, had been in New York, I had visited her a few times in the hospital, had met the husband, but never Simone. Rumor had that she and

43

her son-in-law had been feuding. Arkin was in no condition to deal with Simone's craziness. And crazy she was, I suppose, a workaholic before her daughter's death as well as after, just as Laura, herself pale-white of the purest Victorian sort, her long light-brown hair spread upon the pillow about her narrow face (her face more beautiful than her mother's), had her own craziness, speaking a mile a minute about her doctors, the operation, laughing at Arkin's lewd jokes, told to keep her spirits up (so lewd and spoken with such a leer, with such relish, that I thought he was attacking me in some way, perhaps because I had, with all good motive, broken into their privacy), predicting recoveries, or projecting disasters, new piano pieces to learn, new Chinese recipes to try (Arkin had taken to experimenting with the wok), new eighth-graders to smother with such personal concern that it was overwhelming. Thank God, I thought, there were no young children of their own involved. I drifted away into motherhood. She drifted away. Period.

Perhaps I myself had misremembered everything, though Simone had not, going over every detail with me, culminating with frequent flights to London, flying back to the States and Columbia to teach her classes, then returning to stand by the bed, to clutch her daughter's hands, to goad the nurses, to do battle with her son-in-law, to retreat, finally humiliated by inevitability. No more daughter and mother head to head with competitive brilliance (Mirror, mirror on the wall, Who's the most intellectual of them all?) where no husband could, his silk shirt unbuttoned to the waist, caress her.

"He's leading the life he always wanted to lead now," she said, no longer looking at me, "decided he was gay."

As we approached the tollbooth to the Triborough Bridge, the cab veered away from the change-takers and pulled over to the service road.

Simone tensed. Perhaps she had been victimized by unscrupulous cab drivers before. "What's happening here?" she demanded.

"Tire," he said. "I have to check the tires." He got out of the car and walked carefully around the car. It was still raining. Lightly. Simone watched his every move. I memorized the name and picture on the license taped over the glove compartment. Muhammed Zoutendijik. The odds of getting a native-born cab driver were probably 1,000 to 1. The odds of finding a driver who truly knew his way around were higher than that.

I looked at my watch. "I just want to go home," I said. To no one in particular.

"Who's looking after your children?"

"They're in Brooklyn with their father. I'll get them next weekend."

She tapped her knuckles lightly on the thick plastic shield. "He should at least turn the meter off."

"Or give us credit." How spiritually refreshing it is sometimes to be completely pragmatic.

Mr. Zoutendijik opened the front door and leaned in. "Flat tire," he said. "I have to change it." There were terrible deep lines under his eyes.

"What about us?" There was such an edge to my companion's voice that it even took me by surprise.

"If you ladies please get out, I shall change the tire," Mr. Zoutendijik said. "So sorry, but what can I do?" He shrugged. For the first time I saw his face. His teeth were bad. He was a very short man, slightly more than five feet, with curly hair graying in spots. Swarthy. His manner was not unpleasing, nor even impolite. We were merely in no mood to deal with inconvenience. Hadn't I been trapped in the airport in Pittsburgh for four hours because my original plane had been taken out of service?

"It's raining out," Simone said. "I'm not going to stand out in the rain at two in the morning."

"I give you my umbrella." Mr. Zoutendijik plucked a tattered black umbrella off the floor.

"I don't want your umbrella. I want you to get us another cab right this instant." She was raging at the poor man.

"Please, Miss . . . it will only take a few minutes."

"It's late. I don't have a few more minutes."

"I am an expert at changing tires. World Champion." Realizing that he would have a better chance with me than with Simone, Mr. Zoutendijik crossed to my side and opened the door. I understood that he did not want to lose a good fare. "You and your friend can stand under the roof over there." He pointed to a small concrete building where the police were. "Here. Take my umbrella. No time at all. No time at all."

"My son has cerebral palsy," I said, staring straight ahead, my voice barely audible. Mr. Zoutendijik stood stiffly by the door, holding the umbrella like a chauffeur. Perhaps he had been a chauffeur at some time. Who knows? Anything was possible. Simone didn't say anything. She reached toward my briefcase and took my hand. "Let's get out of the car," she said.

"Only five minutes," Mr. Zoutendijik pleaded. "Only five minutes. I'll adjust the fare."

"You should turn the meter off," Simone said. She still held my hand.

"I'll make adjustments. Promise." He left us under the eaves of the concrete station and trotted back to the cab. I looked down at my free hand and saw that I was carrying my briefcase. How foolish, I thought.

"We must not give up hope," Simone said. We watched Mr. Zoutendijik. He was very efficient in removing the tools from the trunk, allowing the jack to fall to the pavement with a clatter. How tortured he seemed.

"No, we must not give up hope," I said, but both of us were staring into other lives. "Before I left on my trip, Julia, my daughter, came to me to tell me a dream. At first she didn't want to tell me all of it, but before I left she relented. I was in bed, but her father wasn't beside me. Another woman was. And then a man came in and I started to fight with him and scratch him. I jumped out of bed and placed a bag over his head and put him in the closet. Then Julia asked me how we were going to get our clothes out, and I told her that I would put them in

46

another one. I opened the closet wide enough to reach in to get my clothes but not wide enough to let the man out. Julia and I took the clothes and slammed the closet door shut. And then she woke up."

Mr. Zoutendijik was putting the bolts onto the new tire. He had been right. He had not lied to us.

Simone nodded. Our daughters were out of reach, and we did not understand them. Three empty taxis entered the toll plaza, and I knew what Simone was thinking, but all her belongings were in the backseat of Mr. Zoutendijik's cab. To get her attention I said, "One dream triggers another."

"So true," she said, from wherever she was. One could imagine between the streetlights and the sky an angel or two to fill in the great spaces. Mr. Zoutendijik held his hands over his head, like a boxer in triumph, doing a little dance around his battered taxi. What was true of big-city taxis was true for the passengers as well: most of the shocks were gone. "Come, come," Mr. Zoutendijik cried. "All ready. Everything tip-top."

"What else can go wrong tonight?" Simone asked.

"After Julia left to feed her brother, I remembered a dream of my own," I told her. "It was the closest to dying I have ever been. It was a death dream. A dream telling me that I was dying. I was in this large house and there was this party going on. I saw the people filing in one by one, taking their place at the dining-room table. I knew that they had come to mourn me. And I kept struggling to wake up. 'I must stay alive for my children!' I cried. 'I must stay alive for my children!' And when I awoke I cannot tell you how relieved I was. I had been reborn."

"I don't know what it is like to be reborn," Simone said. She climbed into the cab ahead of me. I believe she had been concerned the whole time about leaving her briefcase in the cab whereas I had carried mine with me. Mine filled to the brim with papers not worth saving. "I simply put one foot before the other."

47

"It's one way to get where you are going."

The meter was reading over thirty dollars. Neither of us liked that at all.

As we entered Manhattan, I saw a bag lady huddled in a doorway, sleeping with all her possessions wheeled about her in a shopping cart. No matter how far away from home you travel, you always return to your deepest fears.

Simone placed her briefcase upon her lap and snapped it open. At first I thought that her distrust of Mr. Zoutendijik was so complete that she wanted to make certain that he had not stolen anything from her. On top of her papers was the French book she had been reading.

"I want to show you what that ex-son-in-law of mine has done," she said. "This book." Over thirty dollars to get back to a city one did not wish to live in anymore.

"What is it?"

"*Merité des Femmes.*"

"He wrote it?"

"No."

It did not look like a new book. She held the book, but held it very gently. She waited for me to open my hands.

"I shall deduct four dollars from the fare," Mr. Zoutendijik announced.

"More than that," Simone countered.

"Translated it?"

"No."

"Who wants to be let off first?" Mr. Zoutendijik asked, as we headed west. West!

"The cover," Simone said, allowing two fingers to rest gently on the title.

"It's beautiful." I was not at all certain what kind of response she wanted.

Then back to me. "The skin. The book is bound in Laura's skin."

"What?"

Simone nodded. "It's true. As soon as Laura died, he had the skin of her shoulders removed and taken to a bookbinder. The result is this volume. He doesn't know I have taken it yet."

"How could he do that?"

"Who? Arkin?"

"Yes. Arkin." I felt I had no right to hold the volume for so long. I passed it back to her. Click went the briefcase.

"Oh, he couldn't do it without her permission of course. It had all been worked out ahead of time. She wanted to give the skin he loved so greatly."

"What's he going to do when he finds out you have taken it?"

"I don't know. I don't care," she said.

"Who wants to be let off first?" Mr. Zoutendijik repeated.

"I'll get off first." Simone told him the address. "You know the other day I was in a coffee shop near Columbia and there was a man in there who had suffered a stroke. He was in a wheelchair waiting for his wife or significant other to return from making a phone call, and he kept looking at me, looking at me, trying to say something. He spoke and I couldn't understand him. It was very embarrassing. This sound emanated from his lips but I couldn't make it out. I just kept smiling and nodding and smiling. And finally I understood. Sam. He was saying Sam. His name. So I told him mine. And he smiled at me." She paused. We watched the cab turn onto West End Avenue. "All that effort simply to speak his name." She was changing the subject. But sometimes you have to let people do that.

edna
st. vincent
millay
meets
tarzan

All afternoon I had confused Dorothy
Parker with Edna St. Vincent Millay. I
had done worse than that. I had confused Edna St. Vincent Millay with her
own goddamn self, by which I mean to
say that I kept referring to her as Saint
Edna Vincent Millay. In spite of many
sins, both of omission and commis-
sion, my Catholic boyhood had caught
up with me, along with two vodka
sours. Out of nowhere, a brand new
poet came into being, one with a gold
halo shoved down around her short
black hairs. Saint Edna Vincent Millay!
Good God! What was the canoniza-
tion process coming to?

I definitely was off-balance. It was a Friday afternoon twelve years ago, and some punk and puke-ridden community college had invited me to their campus for a combination interview and crucifixion. All I had to do was bare my soul, promise to give up my firstborn male child, eat dirt, crawl on my belly, and in return, for a half-hour of humiliation heaped upon my hapless head, I would be guaranteed a part-time job for zero dollars an hour. No wonder that I had spent the better part of the early afternoon downing vodka sours. I hate whiskey sours.

To the delight of some eight or nine literary sailors, all of whom were engaged in flying their academic flags at full-mast, I had confused Millay and Dorothy Parker. One of them had spent a good part of her bitter life rubbing elbows with Alexander Woollcott, and Woollcott was such a eunuch, I said, that rubbing elbows with him was about the only part of his anatomy some broad would dare to touch. Finally some Grande-dame of the Lost Generation asked me what I do to encourage freshmen to write themes, and I said, "Pay them." There was quite a silence after that, and soon I was shown to the door. From the ice in the chairman's voice, I knew that I had been condemned to a lifetime of wasted Friday afternoons. I would be the academic equivalent of the Wandering Jew. Without a name I would wander from pillar to post, from post to pillar, from civilization to jungle, until some wild animal stuck forth her head and took pity upon me.

I drove back to Manhattan, parked my car, and walked over to First Avenue and 34th Street. I was tempted to visit a local pub, tempted to put the finishing touches upon my vodka-soured edges, but I decided to punish myself for my failure. What examinations I had taken, I had forgotten, but I had never forgotten what arms lay beneath my head till morning. There were never that many arms to remember. Unless one slept with an octopus. Octopi had numerous arms to remember.

As I climbed the five flights of stairs to my two-and-a-half-room apartment, housing for the once one-and-a-half inhabitants, there was a young woman sitting on the steps near my door. I was quite surprised to see anyone waiting for me, especially a woman whom I had met only once in my life. And in another city. Ah, the whore is dead, but that's another country. Or some such literary allusion. From her posture, I judged she had been waiting for me a long time, and it was quite cold in the hallway. Perhaps she had been napping, and my footsteps had awoken her. A French woman whom I had met through mutual friends.

She wasn't the first person to sleep in the hallway of my building, and so no one had disturbed her. She was certainly much more attractive than the bums who moved up from the Bowery to piss on the hall radiators, sending a stomach-churning fragrance through the building. The young woman wore glasses, reminding me of a joke by Millay. Or was it Parker? Or Ogden Nash? Or Shakespeare? Or Sir Arthur Conan Doyle? What was her name? Men don't make passes, etc.

"I bet you're surprised to see me here," she said, leaping up. She wore a full-length cloth coat and no hat.

"No," I lied. "I expected you all the time. What took you so long to get here?"

My answer took the wind out of her sails. Her shoulders sagged a bit. It was a mean thing for me to do, but suppose I had made other plans for the evening? Suppose I had climbed those five filthy flights of stairs with another woman on my jaundiced arm? What then? What would I have done? What would she have done? Or suppose I hadn't come home at all? Would she have spent the entire night sleeping outside my door? Ah, sweet Metaphysics. As I put the key into the lock and threw the bolt, I knew that my apartment, with its paperback books piled upon each windowsill, with my mattress on the bedroom floor, with papers of all shapes and sizes scattered across two and a half rooms, with the bathroom sitting right next to the gray card table that served as my dining room table, with the sink piled high with unwashed dishes, would not overwhelm this woman with its understated elegance. I was too old to be avant-garde. It all came down to lack of order in my life.

As we stepped inside, Michelle removed two thin steaks from her paper sack. "See," she said, with the correct note of triumph, "we don't even have to go out to eat." She went into the living room, deposited her large handbag on the floor, and took her coat off. "Do you like pepper steaks?"

"Sure," I said, looking for a coat hanger. I found one next to Alberto Moravia's *The Empty Canvas*. The blurb on the paperback read: 'The widely acclaimed new novel by Italy's greatest writer—the story of an artist's sexual bondage to an amoral young girl." Perhaps some unknown publicity writer for Signet Books was trying to tell me something. At least I had hopes.

I had lied about the pepper steaks. I had no idea what she was talking about. All I knew was that I had a can of pepper. Pepper and peanut butter. I was tempted to make a joke about the state of my cupboard and the contents of my refrigerator, but then I remembered that I was dealing with a foreigner. I decided to show her my serious side.

Mouche came out to greet us. Mouche, short for Scaramouche, was my cat. I was fond of Mouche, the way one might be fond of any living thing that shared your grief. Mouche had, however, three annoying habits: she would eat, she would shit, and, every once in a while, she would jump from the top of the bedroom bureau onto my chest. She would perform this last-named kamikaze act in the middle of the night, and the thump on my chest would always scare the living daylights out of me, and at that period in my life there wasn't that much daylight in me. My wife had abandoned me for a clarinet player. I had lost my teaching job. And I had lost a good part of my savings account. A woman I had slept with had gotten pregnant, and I had to give her six hundred dollars so that she could finance an abortion in Philadelphia. I was getting fond of Philadelphia. The City of Brotherly Love. And I had grown fond of my cat, but there are times in a person's life when even owning a cat becomes too heavy a responsibility. That was the kind of time I was in, and Mouche sensed it. Mouche got even by jumping on my chest in the middle of the night. Perhaps this woman would do the same thing.

Did I say the woman with the steaks was named Michelle? Maybe it wasn't her name. But since she was French, maybe it had to be. I had met Michelle through friends in Philadelphia. She and her boyfriend had stayed at my friends' house one night, and they told me they had returned home to find Michelle and her friend romping nude in the snow in their backyard. I wasn't there. I had only heard the reports secondhand.

I placed some candles on the card table and lit them. I located a bottle of wine under the sink. I opened a super brand of cat food for Mouche. I knew it was super because on occasions I had eaten it myself.

Michelle worked as a nurse in a Philadelphia hospital, and she was divorced. I was in the process of getting divorced. We were both the same age, twenty-five, twenty-six, going on a hundred, but I knew she had seen more of life than I had. After all she had been in Paris. I had traveled only as far as Philadelphia, and look at the trouble it was getting me into. The incident about Saint Millay and Sinner Parker was fast fading from my mind. Over dinner, we trotted out our life stories. Because of her accent, I had to listen carefully. I really had not learned to listen to other people very well.

Michelle had married an American GI and he was fond of the movies, especially drive-in movies. He was stationed somewhere in the South, and they would spend their evenings going to drive-in movies. He loved Tarzan movies, and Michelle hated them. She would fall asleep, and then her husband would get very angry, and they would fight, and then she would climb out of the car and hitchhike home. One night two high school boys picked her up, and she brought them home and painted their bodies with bright blue fingerpaints. Her marriage took a turn for the worse after that. There was a wild streak in her that I found most attractive.

"You don't like Tarzan movies?" I asked.

"They're boring," she said.

I told her about drive-in movies in Dania, Florida. On Sunday nights my parents would push my sisters and me into our car, and off we would go to the drive-in. The drive-in was far out of town, in the middle of nowhere, and was located by the side of a river, so quite often the place would be crawling with mosquitoes. Between double features, a truck would pass between the automobiles and cover everything with DDT. We had to roll up the windows to keep the spray from our eyes and lungs, but it was always hot and humid, and with five people in the car with the windows up, the heat became unbearable.

The best part of the Florida drive-in, however, happened when the films were over. The ground was covered with land crabs that had crawled up from the riverbank. It was a great thrill for my sisters and myself to hear the automobiles run over the shells. The cracking and crunching of the shells sounded like tiny firecrackers going off.

"I especially liked the Tarzan movies," I said. "Because watching all the land crabs made me feel as if I had been in the jungle." I had spent many hours as a child practicing my Tarzan yell.

"I don't want to hear it," Michelle said.

After such intimate exchanges, I had naturally assumed that we would sleep together, so I went into the bedroom to make the room presentable. A mattress on the floor and a huge bulletin board covered with unpaid bills and lists of unread books could not conceivably strike any woman as the height of elegance. It was a room in search of a rebellion.

Michelle stayed in the living room for a long time. Perhaps she had changed her mind about spending the night with me. Playing the part of the perfect gentleman, I went out into the living room and told her that I would sleep on the couch and that she could have the bed.

"That won't be necessary," she said. "I was just looking at the lights of the city."

And so we went to bed. She was very passionate, but we were still strangers to one another. Someone said that men tend to fall in love more easily than women. Perhaps it was true. Perhaps everything in the world was true. There were no lies anywhere.

The next morning it was still snowing. We spent the morning in Central Park. An ex-colleague of mine had given me a cap made of Irish wool. He had purchased it through a mail-order catalogue, and when the cap arrived it did not please him, and so he gave it to me. It was his bumbling way of making up for all the cowardice he had shown by not supporting me for tenure. I called it the three-hundred-thousand-dollar cap. I gave it to Michelle. She looked much better in it than I ever would.

We held hands and ran under the overpasses. She made snow angels for me, and I took photographs. She was not what I would call beautiful, but she was very attractive. She had clear blue eyes. We stood in the falling snow and kissed, but now that she was dressed, her body seemed very far away from mine. I tried very hard to be happy.

Against my own best judgment, I insisted that we walk over to the Algonquin Hotel and have a drink. And, of course, when I entered the Algonquin, the entire Millay/Parker debacle spilled back into my life. Not only was I mixing business with pleasure, I was mixing my metaphors. I had, however, made up my mind about the puke college. Even if they, through the grace of God, decided to offer me the job, I would turn it down. I was in a mood to turn the entire world down. How much better in life, I thought, to find a woman one could love, crawl into bed with her, and let life pass on by. Better to fuck one's brains out than to be fucked over by every two-bit sonuvabitch who had a nothing-for-nothing job to hand out. Jobs? There would be other jobs. There was always work in the world to do and to be done by.

"What's the matter?" Michelle asked, holding her Bloody Mary in front of her like a small crystal ball. We looked into it and saw a bright alcoholic future.

"Nothing," I lied. "I was just thinking about all the great people who used to come to this place. Have you ever heard of the Algonquin Round Table?"

"No," she said.

"The Round Table was composed of a lot of wits, or people who thought they were witty, or people who had devoted their lives to acting witty. It is a terrible burden. Wit. It's not worth a plug nickel. It's not like telling the truth to somebody. I mean there were people who struggled to put into the world real work, poems and stories and plays that required sweat and tears and sacrifice. People who devoted their lives to trying to do something worthwhile, and all these people did was sit around trying to hurt one another, acting cruel."

"Like who?" she asked.

"Edgar Rice Burroughs," I told her. "He used to sit around here telling jungle jokes about Tarzan."

For a moment I thought she was going to cry. "That's not true," she said.

I paid the bill and we left the cozy mahogany warmth of the Algonquin. It was still snowing, and I was working very hard at being a New Yorker.

"Don't you like me?" she asked.

"Of course, I like you. I was merely teasing you."

"I don't like to be teased."

"I don't blame you." I still retained the image of her falling asleep at the drive-in movies and I couldn't shake it. I walked her to the train station, and tried to build an elaborate analogy about jungles, about the city as a jungle, and how it was one thing to be alone in the jungle, to be a man among animals, and yet that it was quite another thing to be alone in the city. I tried to expand the idea, but I was merely showing off.

"Are you lonely?" she asked.

"Sometimes," I said. "I was most alone yesterday when I was being interviewed by a half-dozen people."

"I like the Algonquin," she said.

"The next time you come back, we'll take a room there." It sounded good to say it. I didn't have more than six dollars in my pocket, and some of that was earmarked or cat-marked for Mouche.

"Dorothy Parker once co-authored a play called *Ladies of the Corridor,*" I said, feeling very much like the teacher that, deep down, I was, "about single, widowed, or unmarried women, and how they sat in their rooms, or waited in the lounge, or how they nervously paced the corridors, listening for the sounds of life from other rooms, waiting for love to walk up to them and take them by the hand and lead them out of their vast carpeted deserts. Ever since my wife left me, that's the kind of feeling I've had, but maybe the loneliness of men and the loneliness of women have nothing in common with one another. I have a friend who insists that men and women are two different species and that they don't even belong on the same planet together."

Michelle took my hand and we waited for her train. She told me about being a young girl in Paris, about growing up poor, and how she had to scavenge for food. There had been so many children in her family that her parents finally put her in an orphanage. The boys in the orphanage were big and they used to play war games and they frightened her. It frightened her to be treated like an orphan. Once you grow up frightened, she told me, you never get brave again. I knew what she meant.

The train came. We kissed goodbye. "What lips my lips have kissed, and where and why . . ." When she returned to Philadelphia, I called her. I called her two or three times and invited her back. I reminded her about our date at the Algonquin. But she made excuses. I stopped calling. A year later, I came across a copy of *Tarzan and the Apes* and I mailed it to her, along with a book of comic verses by Dorothy Parker. After a few weeks, the package came back. The post office had stamped it: "Moved. No Forwarding Address." We never saw each other again.

roma

1.

Roma. And the thieves were already hard at work. Justin's travelers checks had been lifted from his coat pocket, and his wife's handbag had been slit open, the contents carried off by a gang of twelve-year-olds. As if that had not been enough, an older and more established gang had started a fire near the American Embassy on Via Veneto, and when the fire chief had gone to the scene, thieves broke in and robbed the fire chief's house. Now that was a class act. Smart thinking. Smart thinking had to be rewarded somewhere, even in the city where the summer heat was stifling.

Roma. Justin Bromley never thought he and his wife, Hanley, would ever reach it. Would ever make any journey beyond North Carolina with the smell of sawdust in the air, beyond the lives of their two grown children (with one child dead, a daughter named Hanley, age eleven). In light of the fiasco in the furniture factory, Justin was especially skeptical about going on vacation, even if it was, at best, a working one.

Justin had, as a favor to a client who had kept up ties with Marcos, imported tonqum, a dark wood resembling English oak. As soon as they started to handle the lumber, all the workers in the factory fell prey to asthmatic-like allergies and broke out in rashes. It was a disaster, a lunatic small-town hick plague, with furniture workers collapsing, blacks and whites together coughing, coughing, destroying their lungs. The mistake had almost cost Bromley his furniture business, a business he had put twenty-five years of his life into. One should learn never to do favors. Favors always backfired. And he still had the rash to prove it. No more tonqum. I can't lose any more business, Bromley thought. I don't have enough of a cushion to fall back on.

In Rome, with his marriage dead and dying. How many months had it been since he and Hanley had made love, had engaged in sex, had played the beast with two backs? How many? Three? Four? Who cared even enough to count? Hanley was now walking ahead of him, she of the straight back, her long red hair under an expensive green scarf, her lovely pale-white skin, her guidebooks in hand, her sunglasses pushed to the top of her head, the way a movie star might do it, onto the steps of the Goldoni. Two characters in search of six characters.

"Desidero prenotare due posti per lo spettacolo di venerdi sera?" she said to the woman behind the cage.

He still couldn't believe it. Roma. Across the street from their hotel, on the evening of their arrival, there was a film crew at work. That was what one missed by living in a small town, where the only culture was what the colleges imported from the

North. But now, in a different and more foreign world, he and Hanley could stand on their balcony and peer across into the lights, camera, action. Hundreds of long cables, huge arc lights, and grotesque atmosphere people.

"What were they filming?" he had asked the concierge, but she didn't know. A ghost story, she thought. She was the friend of someone working on the film, though. A man named Genius. He held seances. Would he and the signora be interested in meeting him? Bromley shook his head. Afraid not, he said. I did not come here to play footsies with ghosts. What could anyone make of a person named Genius?

"No matter," the woman had insisted, "there will be a party I shall invite you to. You can make up your minds then. A nice party for theater people. In a big villa not far from here. Some of the film people will be there too. It will be very nice. You can make up your own minds."

Just another scene going on that Bromley did not understand, would never understand. His daughter-in-law, Susan, had said that he should try new things, not be so afraid, but furniture he understood. And food. Sleep when it came. And happiness when it came. If it ever came. Though he didn't understand the process of making films, he had felt, and perhaps Hanley had also felt, happy watching strangers make a film in a language they did not speak. Why not? What unhappiness could it bring? To them, the observers, the devourers of Gamberi, the tourists? The dead ones from the neck down. Happiness was a language too they did not speak.

Susan had called from Charlotte to check on their arrival, to advise them on what to see, advise them about the metropolitana, if it was absolutely necessary to use it. Good girl, Susan. Why she had ever married Harold, Bromley's eldest, Bromley never understood. Harold was good-looking enough, but he was a dedicated CPA and as dull as dishwater. Susan had given them news of Bromley's ex-wife, Diane. They were all still friends. Hanley didn't mind.

Diane's mother was in the hospital with a heart attack. Diane had rented a car and had driven up to Maryland. She was very upset, Diane was, and very alone, and Susan advised Bromley to call her (Diane) and at least leave a message on the tape. Where do we go from here? Back to the hotel room, with another night of watching soccer? After their daughter had died, they had gone nearly two years without touching.

The Corso Vittorio Emanuele. Everything in Rome was so old, so historical, so set out against the sky like a lesson to be memorized. Diane had suggested that he and Hanley visit the little church where Christ had appeared to St. Peter, but she was becoming too religious, too fanatical. He and Hanley had ignored the sermon. Besides, was it not true that once a traveler left home, miracles were everywhere? Miracles for the asking. The hour of the Ave Maria.

"What's the matter?" Hanley asked.

"Diane's mother is dying," he said, not really saying anything.

"She's very frail," Hanley said, referring to Diane.

"Yes," he agreed. "She is very frail. Spends half her life going to the doctors. But then she will outlive us all. That's what frail people do. Exhaust us with their frailties and then go on."

Hanley stared at him, curiously, as if to say, who knows these things? Indeed who does?

"Did you get the tickets?" he asked.

"Yes," she said. "I did. For Friday night."

Friday night with Pirandello. What more could anyone ask? Rent a car, drive out of town, explore some district where no one dared go.

Their daughter had wanted to be an actress, but some things are not meant to be. If you live long enough, Bromley concluded, everything is stolen from you. He turned toward the American Express office. Three months earlier, thieves had gained access to his telephone charge card and had rung up over three thousand dollars' worth of phone calls to Colombia and Honduras. Drug rings everywhere, but at least the phone company had been understanding about his plight. As if someone might show sympathy for the plight of innocents beset by thieves. One could not be too careful.

"You're not going up to see the factory this weekend?" she asked.

He shrugged. "I have to visit a factory or two. For tax purposes," he added.

2.

O Dolce O dolce vita mia.
O dolce
O dolce vita a mia.

The voices were going up to God. Yes, they were. Standing in the shadow of the church of Santa Maria di Monserrato, the more Justin thought about the face of the actress in the movie being filmed across the street from their hotel, the more the woman reminded him of Hanley—not his wife, but his daughter. The actress, with her close-cropped blonde hair, her blue eyes, the severe way she had of carrying herself, always majestic, never slouching. Hanley, carrying a John Buchan novel, appeared next to him. He had never understood her tastes. She seemed to be mocking his own taste in reading materials. A Walt Disney comic book in Italian. *Almanacco Topolino.* A gift for their grandchild. Besides, Justin thought it would be a good way to learn the language. Un tempo cosi e l'ideale per un bagno. His granddaughter was very fond of Mickey Mouse. And swimming.

Hanley seemed to materialize out of nowhere, but always with a book in her hand. They stood side by side in the night, listening.

O dolce vita mia.

Che t'haggio fatto.

Justin placed his hand on her bare arm. She moved her arm away.

3.

"And so you know these things about life?" the concierge had said earlier that morning, giggling, putting her hand to her mouth. A woman of about seventy with white hair, almost three hundred pounds of her, without teeth, the body mass of a small planet. "You will come to the after-theater party, won't you? Some of the film people will be there too. A great treat. Some very big stars."

"But we don't know anybody," Hanley said.

"I only know Topolino," Justin added, smiling.

The concierge waved them away. "It does not matter. You come to Rome to make new friends. Why else travel? Old friends you have at home. These are very exciting people. Theater people. They hardly listen when you talk to them. Oh but they are gorgeous to look at. I can arrange all the transportation."

She must be in need of extra money, Justin thought.

And now he turned. And then he saw her. His daughter, Hanley, standing in Via della Foce, smiling, floating. He ran toward her calling her name, and she was gone, and his wife, who was buying cigarettes, thinking that he was calling her, had turned her attention toward him. She became confused. When he did not answer her, she became annoyed. When he returned to her, he did not look changed. He did not say what he had seen. *Fantastico.*

Where was the street, he asked, that led to the house of Cupid?

Between the Temple, someone said.

"Have you decided to visit the factory?" Hanley asked.

"No, I haven't," he said, noticing that his hands were trembling. "Why do you keep asking me? Do you want to get rid of me? Not that it matters, I guess."

"But we have tickets to see *Il giuoco delle parti*," she said.

"I know all about the tickets," he answered with anger. "I was there when you bought them. Remember?

64

Remember? Perhaps she had fallen in love with someone else. Why not? Anything was possible. Except, of course, what was controlled by Fate or by one's character. Or by one's lack of character. I lack character, Bromley thought. I always have. That is why my own wife doesn't sleep with me.

4.

"Let me tell you," the actress with the close-cropped blonde hair said to Justin. She was standing very close to him so that he felt surrounded by her perfume. The theater party was in full swing, and Hanley was dancing with one of the actors, a tall thin man, with thin hair and a pasty white face. "I was staying on this kibbutz in Israel, and I decided to organize an evening of World War II songs. You know, some British songs, some American songs, some Italian songs. There was a man on the kibbutz who was an expert on them, could sing them all, in their original languages. So I get some more singers together to help with the choruses, that sort of thing, I hung the lights, I designed the sets, and we're about halfway through the rehearsal when the sirens go off, announcing that the Arabs had breached the outer perimeter, had cut their way through the fence.

"In a few minutes, helicopters and planes were flying over our theater, and the planes were dropping flares. All the while, we're singing World War II songs, you understand. We were all laughing, because it could not have been more appropriate.

"But it turned out that some of the flares had been dropped from too low a height, and so they went off on the ground in the middle of the wheat field. Soon the whole field was in flames, and everybody on the kibbutz had to be called out to fight it. There I am, in the middle of rehearsal, and my singers are running this way and that way. All I could do was laugh. I mean it was horrible, of course. What with the fire and the terrorists trying to shoot their way into our camp. . . . Why are you staring at me like that?"

"I'm sorry," Justin said. "I didn't realize I was staring."

"You were."

Perhaps his wife would go off with someone else and where would he be? She had tried it before. Or had she? Some things were impossible to understand.

"You look so much like my daughter," he said at last, taking another glass of wine from a tray being carried through the room. He would get drunk. Perhaps that would cover his embarrassment. He was grateful he had found someone to speak English with.

"Do I?" the actress asked, opening her large blue eyes. She was short, animated.

"Yes."

"Where is she? Is she here with you?"

"Yes," he said, and then, looking away, he changed his mind. Too difficult to explain. "She died a few years ago."

"Oh. I am very sorry," the actress said. Embarrassment crossed her face.

"Yes," he said, weakly. "A car accident."

"Was she very young?"

"Yes," he said, staring into the wine. "She was very young. Eleven. I think she had her heart set on being an actress."

"I am sorry," the actress said. She touched him lightly on the arm. "But perhaps she is blessed. Being an actress is a terrible thing."

"Is it?" Where was Hanley? He couldn't see her. Had she stepped out onto the balcony with her dancing partner? The room, as large as it was, was crowded and hot. The performance of *Il giuoco delle parti* had been a great success and the men and the women in the room were noisy and self-congratulatory, with much embracing and kissing.

"I wouldn't wish it on anyone."

"What will play next?"

"*Riders to the Sea* by Synge. Do you know it?"

"No." He could feel his cheeks redden. Terrible always to be so foolish. So small-townish. "It's my wife who loves the theater. That's why we have been so infatuated, watching you from our hotel."

"Ah!" Her blue eyes brightened. "You mean the movie?"

"Yes, the movie. What is it about? My wife and I have been watching you film some of the scenes in the Piazza." He paused. He realized he was repeating himself.

"I don't know what it is about really," the actress said, shaking her head sadly. "I only have a few scenes, and the director is very secretive. Too much improvisation, I think, but as far as I can tell, it is something about a woman who thinks her husband is unfaithful and so she consults with the spirit world to gain evidence against him. And when she gains the proof she needs, she becomes free of him. It seems like fun, but it is so boring, standing around, waiting to do your scene, then go home."

"You seem to know more than you admit," Justin said, craning his neck, looking for Hanley, spotting her near one of the food tables. His shirt was becoming sweat-stained under the arms.

"Yes," the actress said, nodding to her friends. "I think that is true for all of us, isn't it? We know more than we admit. My husband says that film-making is merely a mirror image for life. We stand around waiting to do our scenes and then go home." She laughed at her own jest, a laughter so much like the laugh of his daughter that it caused him to wince.

"Or if it is like life," he added, picking up his cue, "the director is too secretive and there is too much improvisation."

The actress liked that one. She laughed loudly. A free spirit in paradise.

He sensed, perhaps incorrectly, that she wanted to get free of him, but he didn't want to release his prisoner. Suppose there would be no one else to talk to?

And the hostess made an announcement in a language he did not understand.

"What did she say?"

"Oh, someone is going to be hypnotized," the actress said. "Come, come, we must go upstairs and see. It will be great fun.

It is amazing what people do. They take off their clothes and cackle like chickens." She took Justin by the hand and led him up a wide and graciously curving marble staircase. Whoever was throwing the party was wealthy. Very wealthy. Bromley looked at the well-carved furnishings with envy. His own furniture was well made, but it had to be economical, affordable. How much better it would be to build without worrying about the cost or one's workers breaking out in rashes. How wonderful it would be to live without ever once considering the cost. Or was that impossible? Why wish if one wished only for what was possible? Good wood. Bad wood. What wood would one build Pinocchio's nose out of? Tonqum, of course. From the top of the stairs, he could look down on Hanley's red hair and the crowd around her, admiring her. She was dancing with great animation, clapping her hands. Anything was possible when one viewed it from a great height. He would drop a flare and burn everything in sight.

The sitting room upstairs was packed. Wall-to-wall people. The French doors leading to the terrace were wide open, but there was no breeze. Standing in the middle of the room was a short man with a bald head. Like most every other man in the room, he was wearing a tuxedo. Another man standing in front of him was questioning him.

"Dove sei adesso?"

"Sono in un lebbrosario."

"Cosa succede nel lebbrosario?"

"Mia moglie si sta togliendo le tette, per mostramele su un vassoio e farmele succhiare."

"Fantastico!"

"What are they saying?" Bromley asked.

"Shhhh!" an older woman, witchlike in her domain under the candles, placed her finger to her lips.

The actress took Bromley's hand and squeezed it. She did not answer. Bromley wondered if she was interested in him, if she would sleep with him. But he was afraid of what would happen.

She reminded him too much of what his daughter would have become, had she lived to become an actress herself.

The hypnotist brought forth two melons on a tray. "Show us," he said.

Had she lived. Who could conceive of a more terrifying phrase? From where he stood, he could look through the open door, across the courtyard jammed with parked cars, into the world beyond.

The audience howled.

A woman behind him said, in English, "I was all prepared to sleep with him. Had worked out a plan and told my husband that I was taking the children to visit their grandparents in the city. I called my friend and we agreed to meet at the zoo. There was a hotel near the zoo that I knew we could go to. I was very excited thinking about it. After all, I had been faithful to my husband for nearly twenty years. That was long enough. And you know what happened? My friend went to the wrong zoo. I was waiting at the children's zoo and he was waiting at the main one. We never did meet up."

Bromley turned to find the source of the conversation, the voice being so much like his wife's, to look at the woman in the face. She was younger than Hanley, not nearly so attractive. A tall brunette, with a long cigarette holder and green nail polish. He shuddered.

The hypnotized man was holding the melons, believing they were breasts.

On the terrace, from beyond, the eleven-year-old Hanley was waving to her father.

Hanley smiled at him. Perhaps she was encouraging him to sleep with the actress. It would take the burden of sex from his wife.

It was all melting together now. The mornings. The evenings. The nights. "Like Pirandello," the actress had told him when they met, "I am a child of chaos."

Who isn't? he thought.

"Excuse me," a second hypnotized subject said. "Must I wear the chef's hat?"

"Absolutely," the hypnotist said. "Absolutely." He placed such a hat on the head of his subject. The hypnotized man began to shift and stir.

She took him by the hand and led him back downstairs. In the living room, a plump woman in red was standing on the sofa and lifting her skirts, unbuttoning her blouse, dancing like a gypsy in her bare feet. Hanley was not among the spectators, nor was she still on the dance floor. Nowhere to be seen.

The actress led Justin outside, into a courtyard where the automobiles and limousines were parked. Past two bored chauffeurs who were reading newspapers.

"Have you been drinking as much as I have?" she asked him. "I hope not." She opened her purse and retrieved keys to her car, jingling them. From the villa, Justin could hear singing and dancing and, from upstairs, more laughter as another hypnotized subject was put through his or her paces.

She unlocked a long black car with darkened windows. "Wait," she said. "We can use the back seat. It is very private."

She opened the back door, kicked off her shoes, and slid inside. She lay on her back, her skirt over her hips. She beckoned to him. "Hurry," she said. "While we are all alone."

"Wait," he said. To make certain that he still had his wallet, he touched the pocket of his coat. Suppose this was a trap, he wondered. Maybe there was a man or two lurking in the shadows? Or the chauffeurs pretending to lounge? Maybe to jump on him and steal his wallet? Or to blackmail him?

"See how much room there is in here?" the actress asked. She patted the leather upholstery.

Justin looked around, saw no one but the two chauffeurs, entered the car, and pulled the door shut.

"Lock it," she said. Her hands were already under her black dress, pulling her panties down. She left them on her ankle, lifting her foot up, offering them to him.

Justin sat against the door, the ridge holding the ashtray pressing against the small of his back. "Please," he said, "I'm sorry. I can't."

The actress lowered her foot and raised herself on her elbows. "What do you mean?"

"You remind me too much of my daughter," he blurted out, then started to cry. He hated this, this impotence that had overtaken him. The wind blowing through the trees? What was it saying?

The actress reached toward him and with both arms pulled him down to her breasts. He could feel her nakedness under him. "Poor baby," she said. "Poor, poor baby." She undid his belt and loosed his pants. "Shhh! Everything is going to be all right."

But it wasn't. He pushed open the door and jumped out of the car, his pants about his ankles. He felt like a fool. He was a fool. In the middle of a strange city, his legs still bearing blotches from the rash, he was Topolino trying to zip up under a three-quarter moon. And who was that waving at him at the edge of the courtyard—so young? So young. They take off their clothes and cackle like chickens.

5.

His wife did not return from the party until after two. He imagined the pasty-faced actor had driven her back. When the door to the hotel room opened, he was sitting up in bed, waiting for her.

"Where were you?" he asked. "I looked all over for you."

"I was looking all over for you too," she said, pausing in front of the dresser, kicking off her shoes in the same way the actress had hours before. Hanley removed her long earrings, square hand-painted ones she had purchased in the airport.

"Someone told me you had left," he lied.

"Well, I hadn't."

"With the actor you were dancing with."

"Well, I didn't." She went into the bathroom and left the door open. "What happened between you and Amalia?"

"Amalia? Who's Amalia?" He allowed the pages from the *Herald-Tribune* to slide to the floor. The best thing about living in hotels, he thought, was that there was always someone else around to clean up the mess.

She came out of the bathroom, wearing her slip. "Wasn't that the name of the actress you were with?"

"No," he said. "I don't think so. I think she told me another name."

"Another name?" She sat on the bed and removed her stockings. If she had been making love, Justin thought, would she have bothered to put her stockings back on? It was difficult to know about such things.

"Yes, but I don't remember," he said finally. "Did you go upstairs to watch the hypnotist?"

"No," she said, pulling off her garter belt. "I didn't even know there was a hypnotist."

"Well, I don't see how you could have missed it," he observed dryly.

"I guess I did. What did I miss? Was it funny?" She sat with her legs wide apart as if she was taunting him.

"No. I thought it was humiliating."

"Why? Were you the one hypnotized?"

"No. But I thought it was humiliating. That's all. You want any of the newspaper?"

"No. I'm going to take a shower. Wasn't that villa terribly warm? I thought it terribly warm."

"What about your actor?"

"My actor? Not my actor, dear. Just a nice man. Very funny. Has a brother who found a dinosaur head filled with gold."

"Really?"

"Really."

She went back to the bathroom. After her shower, she changed into her white nightgown. For the first time in a long time, Hanley did not read in bed. The John Buchan book remained unopened on the nightstand.

"Maybe tomorrow I'll drive to Anzio and see the factory."

"Yes," she said. "Maybe tomorrow would be a good time for you to do that."

"Why? Do you have plans?"

"No. I don't have any plans."

6.

The phone rang. The phone! It was terrifying in its insistence. Hanley jumped. Frightened. "Oh no," she cried. "Justin!"

Justin, his heart beating rapidly, reached for the receiver. The little electric clock on the nightstand read three-thirty.

"Who could be calling at this time of night?"

"Hello?" he said into the receiver. To Hanley he said, "Maybe it is somebody from the States who is not aware of the time difference."

The person at the other end of the line was sobbing. "She died!" she blurted out. "Momma's dead!"

"Who is it?" Hanley asked.

"She died before I got there!"

"It's Diane," Justin said. He sat up and switched on the light. "Her mother's dead."

"Justin are you there?"

"I'm here," he said as calmly as he could. He cradled the phone into his neck and searched the nightstand for a cigarette. "Are you all right?"

"They said she was getting better, but when I got there she was dead."

"Where are you?"

"The hospital." She was sobbing. The crying terrified him. It surrounded him in ways he did not understand.

"Where is she?" Hanley asked.

"At the hospital."

"Ask if anyone is there with her, or if she's all by herself."

"Are you by yourself?"

"Yes. I'm alone," she wailed. "I couldn't think of anyone else to call."

"It's all right," he said softly. "I'm glad you called."

Hanley got out of bed and went to the bathroom. Poor Diane was all she said. Poor Diane.

"Where's your brother?" Justin asked.

"He's on his way. He should arrive in a couple of hours. It caught us all off guard. If I had known, I would have driven up last weekend. They were scheduling tests."

If I had known, Justin thought. Another set of frightening words. *If I had known* or *had she lived.*

"Well, maybe it's for the best," he said, fumbling for the phrases that he had used before, or phrases that had been used on him. "She died quickly, with little pain. She lived a long life . . ."

"Not long enough . . ."

"So many people go through long months of needless suffering," he sighed. He lit his cigarette and stared toward the light in the bathroom. When Hanley came out, she said: "Give Diane my love. Tell her I'm thinking of her." She slid back onto the bed, but she did not get under the covers.

"Hanley sends her love," he said, not to Diane but into the receiver, into the object. She didn't sound thousands of miles away. The wonders of technology. "You can call us anytime, you know that."

"I'm in so much pain I can't stand it."

"If things get too bad, call Harold and Susan. I know they'll come up and get you."

Justin let her cry. Then he said, "It's not for us to play God." He talked to her for about twenty more minutes, then hung up. He finished his cigarette.

"Is she all right?" Hanley asked.

"As well as can be expected under the circumstances, I guess."

"Is she close to her brother?"

"No." He lay back down on the bed.

"It's terrible to feel that people go out of your life forever and never come back."

"Yes," he said. They lay together side by side. He reached out and took his wife's hand. She did not move away. He waited, then turned to her, brushing her forehead. She did not move away.

She closed her eyes. He leaned down and kissed her. She did not move away. She opened her mouth. His tongue was inside her. He pushed her nightgown up and caressed her breasts, then held her nipples.

"Wait," she whispered. She had to put her diaphragm in. She got up and went inside the bathroom. Justin waited. He removed his pajamas and enjoyed the hardening of his manhood.

When she returned to the bed, she stood beside him and removed her nightgown, allowing it to fall to the floor. She leaned over him, her breasts touching his chest and then his stomach and then lower. She took him into her mouth, and Justin closed his eyes and sighed. And then, before he came, she came up to his mouth and they kissed for a long time, and then he turned onto the bed and went down on her, inhaling her, pulling lightly at her hair, using his fingers to spread her lips, then his tongue inside her, until she was calling his name over and over, and then entering her and Justin! Justin! she sighed, O God O God, and he thought, to make up for all the times he had been denied, he would stay in her a long time, stroking her, go slow she said, go slow, and he was thrusting harder and harder and deeper, and her body shuddered until she burst into tears and he felt the wetness of her face against his face. We'll fuck all night, he said. Yes, she said. Yes. Come inside me. Then after a while they stopped, and they lay side by side, touching, and she not moving away, his hands lightly over her full breasts, man and wife waiting for morning and the slow awakening of a city called Eternal.

displacements

Ever since my father's death last
March, I have been watching myself as
I play with my three-year-old twin
sons, wondering all the while: Did my
own father play with me in the same
way? Did he say the same things I tell
my sons? Did he hug me the way I hug
them? Sometimes I am standing out in
the sunlight and I think that he can no
longer do that anymore, or as William
Saroyan once said: He no longer ties
his shoes.

But that is a subject for another
story. What I want to write about is
displacement. Displacement is when

76

you start out in one direction in life and end up in another. I know that is not what the term means when psychiatrists employ it. Displacement means something else to them. What it means to me is this: You keep taking it on the chin, and so in order to escape getting slugged, you move further and further away from the punches. Soon you're out of your own life altogether. For example:

I am seated in a Chinese restaurant with a sixty-five-year-old woman who teaches English at a college in Manhattan. Every so often we take turns treating each other to lunch. It is my duty to scout out new restaurants. Since she enjoys Oriental cooking, and since she very rarely eats out, we invariably end up at a Chinese restaurant. The prices are also more reasonable than at other places. I am in my forties and also teach. On teachers' salaries, we're not off to the Four Seasons.

We have been doing these lunches for years, and gradually we have unfolded our lives to one another. Both lives are rather short on excitement, sexual or otherwise.

Before the dessert of green-tea ice cream, Edith says to me: "My older sister has a family album of our growing up in Hoboken. And just the other day as I was looking at the pictures, I noticed something that I had seen before but had not really seen before—every picture shows my sister and me standing on the sidewalk in front of our house—and we're just standing, not moving, not jumping, all dressed up and not going anywhere. And that is exactly how I remember my life. Standing in front of my house, not moving. Not going anywhere. Stiff. Properly dressed. Obedient."

"Our lives are mostly what we think they are," I say, studying the check. It's my turn to treat.

"Precisely," she says. "Precisely."

Fortunes in the fortune cookies are rarely fortunes these days. I crack one open, and on the tiny slip of paper is printed: "A woman who confides to a man that she dreamt that they had intercourse together, or who reveals to him that his mistress quarreled with her because he absentmindedly called her by her rival's name, or who gives him gifts bearing marks made by her own fingers and teeth, or who shamelessly confesses that she is aware that he has desired her for a long time, and asks him who is more beautiful, his mistress or herself, such a person is known as a *go-between who represents her own desires*. The man should meet and converse with such a woman alone and in secret." KAMA SUTRA

"What's it say?" Edith asks, leaving the final spoonful of green-tea ice cream for me.

"I'm not certain," I tell her. "I don't even understand fortune cookies anymore." Too embarrassed to read it to her, I pass her the sheet of paper. After she reads it, she looks up and says, "Precisely."

Three days later I am pissing blood. Nothing frightens me more than to piss blood. It means either I am going to die, or some new kidney stone is going to kick the bejeesus out of me. I sit at my desk, take out some white paper, and start to write my last will and testament. I'm too young to die, but I have no choice.

I am thinking of which books I am going to bestow upon which friend—which friend will be dearly pleased to receive from my dead pulse a copy of Washington Irving's *The Sketch Book*. A first edition. Must be worth something to somebody. A first edition of *Moby Dick* went the other day for $4,000. Doesn't exactly compare to the $125,000 somebody spent for the red shoes worn by Judy Garland in *The Wizard of Oz*, but that's America for you. Capitalism in action. In one of my paperbacks, I notice that Saroyan has written, "Now, I had been brought up in the orphanage according to rules that hadn't yet been displaced." My life is filled with such rules. Your life too, I imagine.

I am thinking that perhaps I should leave Edith something—perhaps my collected Sigmund Freud—when she walks in and sits down. "How are you, Richard?" she asks. Everybody else calls me Dick. She calls me Richard. "Fine," I lie. If I go to the doctor, it's going to cost me more than I can afford. My sons need shoes.

"What is it that separates men from animals?" she asks. She is dressed in a maroon suit with a white blouse. The whiteness of the blouse (I was going to say the whiteness of the whale, but that might give an inappropriate impression of Edith. She is not large. Slender, in fact).

"Regret," I answer, crossing off several names on my list. As one grows older, one's friends fall away. As Robert Redford says in *The Natural,* "Life did not work out the way I had expected." Nor for Edith either, I imagine. I shall leave her some jewelry left to me by my mother.

"Precisely," Edith says, opening her pocketbook and removing a photo of a bearded man in a striped suit. "Have you ever seen this man before?"

Thinking about the blood in my urine, I study the snapshot the way a private detective might. So much of my life has been a pale imitation of movie characters. "No," I tell her.

"It's not a good picture because I took it through my living-room window when he wasn't aware of what I was doing."

"Why?"

"I'm going to tell you why."

Thanks, I think to myself, just what I need when the pain feels something like a dull knife in my right kidney. "Oh . . . Oooh?"

This is what Edith says:

As you know, Richard, my husband died five years ago. The first few months after his death were quite difficult, and you were kind enough to cover my classes. Don't shrug, as if it's nothing. It meant a lot to me then and it means a lot to me now. And because soon I am going to be retiring or forced into retirement, and going back to an empty house, and because we'll very rarely see each other and have few lunches with or without bizarre fortune cookies that tell no fortunes but mock us with their decisiveness, I am going to share something with you that I have not shared with a living soul. No, you need not close the door. It is not sordid. It merely makes me look a bit foolish. And don't look so pained. I'll try to tell it quickly so you won't be bored. I know you. You're always thinking of two or three things at the same time, and I know you have papers to grade. So do I for that matter.

We think we're so smart, but it's amazing how gullible we are when it comes to matters of life and death. And helpless too, helpless, unable to do anything. But two months after Irving's death, the man in the snapshot appeared at my door. . . . Yes, I know you are a step ahead of me. . . . I can tell by the look on your face. . . . Yes, it was the man in the snapshot. He said he had some information that he thought might interest me. He said he had seen Irving in another town. But of course he was a madman. Or charlatan. What else could he be? I had watched Irving's casket being lowered into the ground. Go out to Cowper Cemetery and you can see for yourself that the grave has never been disturbed. I asked for the man's name so I could inform the police in case he had been approaching other widows with his scheme. He said his name was Irving too. Irving Forsgaleon. Not a common name, I should think. Probably a pseudonym. Most likely. . . . Or alias. I guess that's the word I want.

But it was the middle of July, and I really had a lot of time on my hands, and this Mr. Forsgaleon looked quite presentable. His suit was pressed. His shoes were shined. His fingernails were clean and manicured. He was approximately the same age as you, Richard, and so I decided to invite him in. Now don't look so shocked, Richard. I wasn't inviting him into my bedroom, if that's what you're thinking.

And you can wipe that smug expression off your face, because there's a lot about life you don't understand yet. I mean a lot of things happen to a woman when her husband dies, especially if she has been married for over forty years, the way I was.

And why did I invite him in? Because he had a snapshot with him. He pulled it out of his coat pocket and showed me a picture of my late husband driving a Cadillac in a little town called Candlewood. Candlewood. Do you know where Candlewood is? It's in New Jersey. Now first of all, what caused my heart to stop was that Irving, my Irving, was wearing the same suit he had been buried in. And it was a very recent picture, but of course, I had no idea just when the picture was taken. Mr. Forsgaleon claimed it had been taken the week before, but how could he prove it? Also, my husband never owned a Cadillac in his life. He always wanted one, but we never got around to buying one—what with sending the children through college, etc., etc.—and what business would Irving have in Candlewood?

Mr. Forsgaleon said: "Look, I'll leave you the photo for a few days. It's just an ordinary Polaroid. If you think it's a fake or it's been touched up, take it to any expert you want. Any expert will tell you it's authentic. That's your husband. I know where he is. If you want to see him, I'll take you to him."

"For a fee of course," I said.

"I don't deny it," he told me. "I'm in it for the business. I have to make my living like anybody else. So many charlatans around, I have to use every resource at my command to protect my territory."

"What is your territory?" I asked him.

"Me? I am a Vitalogist. A student of life. It's been widely known for years that death is merely an illusion. Nobody dies." Stop making faces, Richard. Of course I thought it was nonsense too. I hate people who deny death. Who run away from reality and make up illusions. Illusions are no comfort. No comfort at all. But there was this terrible snapshot to deal with. It looked so much like my late husband.

But that was not what convinced me to continue talking with him. What convinced me was what he talked about when I invited him inside. If this story is so painful to you, Richard, I need not continue. Are you all right? All right, I'll tell you what

81

he talked about. I invited him into my kitchen, gave him some lemonade, and instead of talking to me about Irving and how much it was going to cost me to get my husband back from some City of the Dead, he started to talk to me about Rip Van Winkle.

Yes, Richard. You heard me right. Rip Van Winkle. He sat at my kitchen table, took out a pocket comb to run through his gray hair, the sunlight falling over him—you remember that scene in *The Natural,* the motion-picture version, I mean? Where Glenn Close is seated in the stands and her hat is lit up and she is the only one shining, meaning something mystical, something beyond understanding?—well, this is what he said:

"Do you know the story of Rip Van Winkle? Of course you do. Everybody does. It's considered a classic. Taught in every high school in the land. At least it was taught in my high school. You're an English teacher, aren't you? Of course you are. I knew that before I came all the way out here. I know it sounds silly, but I might just as well come right out and say it: I come from far, far away. That's how I know where the dead go. When it comes to knowledge of the occult, humans are light-years behind the times. Especially the educated ones. Doubting Thomases, when all about you the miraculous is happening all the time.

"I say I know where your husband is and that I am willing to take you to him, if you so desire, but your only thought is to get enough information about me so you can turn me over to the police. That's why you've invited me in, isn't it? Well, I am going to play on your turf.

"Now let's take Rip Van Winkle, which all you teachers think is some kind of a classic, or why would you bother to make your students read it? And yet, what's it about? Nothing. A man falls asleep and wakes up twenty years later, and everything has changed. So what? What's the big deal? I'll tell you what the big deal is: the real story is what Washington Irving leaves out.

"What people leave out. That's the best part of every story. You have a copy of the story here? Let me show you a few things. I'll be the teacher. You be the student for a change.

"A man goes up into the Kaatskill Mountains and he meets some strange-looking people. Perhaps they are from another planet. At least they're from another time zone. Here it is. The two sentences where the entire story occurs. Sentence one: 'One taste provoked another; and he reiterated his visits to the flagon so often that at length his senses were overpowered, his eyes swam in his head, his head gradually declined, and he fell into a deep sleep.'

"Sentence two starts the next paragraph: 'On waking, he found himself on the green knoll whence he had first seen the old man of the glen.' From sleeping to waking with a paragraph break. From the rest of the story, you would think the most interesting part of the story is how Rip Van Winkle returns home to find everything changed. But that's the least interesting part of the tale. That's the anecdote. It's nothing. It's obvious. Of course things are going to change after twenty years. But suppose he woke up *and found nothing changed—nothing at all!* Now there would be a real tale, one worthy of a master. He would never have known he had slept so long!

"But the most important part of the story is simply passed over. What happened to Rip Van Winkle as he slept? Or did he sleep? Did he remain on the ground in the mountains for the entire twenty years? The author, using the image of the rusted fowling piece, implies that he did: 'He looked around for his gun, but in place of the clean, well-oiled fowling piece he found an old firelock lying by him, the barrel encrusted with rust.'

"But if Rip Van Winkle had been on the ground for twenty years, why was it no one ever stumbled across him? All right, he was in such an out-of-the-way place—say, where the dead visit—that nobody ever climbed there. Only Rip climbed there. Why him? Why is he the chosen? Because he is so lazy? Then it is a punishment? Because he is so beloved by the people of his village? Then it is a reward? Or, more likely, it happens simply because it happens.

"If he slept on the ground for twenty years, what happened during the winter? It wasn't Florida, you know. I bet the winters can get pretty chilly up in the Kaatskills. He would have frozen to death—unless, of course, he was given some supernatural protection? Or, if you allow me to be whimsical, perhaps the magic potion in the cursed flagon was antifreeze.

"Rip Van Winkle either sleeps on the ground, or he does not. If he does not, where was he? Perhaps he was in a time warp, implied by the casual reference in the final sentence of the tale to Hendrick Hudson and his crew playing ninepins. You might argue that he was carried off by that ship and then returned, like Odysseus, twenty years later. In other words, Mrs. Seidman, to put the story in your ball park, what happens to Rip Van Winkle during his long sleep are the struggles of Odysseus.

"Now, if Rip Van Winkle is carried off by some long-dead sailor and then returned, we have a subject that Washington Irving did not have the nerve to deal with. It might just as well be argued that poor old Rip Van Winkle was carried off into a spaceship and taken to another planet.

"Oh sure, we're used to describing visitors from other planets as BEMS, bugged-eyed monsters, if you will (Is Them a Bem?), but why not describe such visitors the way Washington Irving does: 'Their visages, too, were peculiar; one had a large beard, broad face, and small piggish eyes, the face of another seemed to consist entirely of nose and was surmounted by a white sugarloaf hat set off with a red cock's tail.' If that does not sound like a visitor from another planet, then I don't know what does.

"In other words, Washington Irving had hit upon a truth he was unable to deal with, and so he glossed over it. He glossed over it so skillfully that readers rarely understand what the story is about. If Rip Van Winkle had slept, he would have been on the ground for someone to find. If he had slept, he would have frozen to death. If he had slept, he would have starved to death. If he had slept, he would have been unable to stand up.

"But he did not sleep. That is what the story is about."

"And so how could I resist a man like that?" Edith, in all innocence, asks.

84

"Ah!" I cry out.

"Is there anything wrong?"

"No," I gasp. The pain in my lower back is excruciating, but I manage to stand up. I excuse myself. "I'll be right back," I tell her. "Don't go away."

I go the faculty men's room located at the end of the hall. Inside one of the stalls one of my colleagues is seated with his ever-present portable radio on the floor.

I stagger toward the urinal and piss more blood. Why do hospitals and doctors have to be so expensive?

The weatherman on the radio announces: "In essence, when a weather system is unstable, a small displacement leads to a larger one."

If I could displace this kidney stone, I think, I would crawl on my hands and knees to Lourdes. I would give away my collection of children's books to some deserving or even nondeserving orphan. I would give up drinking. I would become a saint. Patron saint of pedants. My sign would be blood in the urine. A sign from God. Surely.

When I came to, I was in the emergency room of St. Luke's Hospital. I didn't get back to work until five days later. All that time I didn't think more than twice about my friend Edith giving away her paltry life-savings to some charlatan—and a rotten Irving explicator at that.

The following week, because I was absurdly behind—and *absurdly* is the correct word—in my paper grading, I had spent most of my evenings in my office.

On Tuesday, three weeks later, Edith turned up. Immaculately dressed as usual, with a floral stickpin in her silk blouse, a pearl necklace, and some bracelets and rings. She was carrying a cardboard box filled with books. "You want any of these college readers?"

"I can do without them, thank you. I imagine the students can too." Out of courtesy, however, I looked through the box and pulled out a tattered copy of *The American Review of*

Reviews because it had an article about the progress of the world. The progress of the world is a subject that is of great interest to me. An illusion, most likely. "What happened to you and Irving?" I asked as casually as I could. "May I have this?"

"Certainly." She sat down in her chair. "Well, as I was trying to tell you the afternoon you disappeared on me, I became quite curious about Irving's line of work, much against my better judgment."

"That's not like you," I said.

"It's not like anyone to be presented with a half-a-dozen snapshots of one's supposedly dead husband driving all over New Jersey."

"Only the dead know New Jersey."

"Or Brooklyn," she added.

"Or Brooklyn. What do the dead do?" I asked, sifting through the dregs of the cardboard box. "Do they drive from town to town? Do they sign up for tours?"

"I'm not going to tell you anything if you're going to be that way," she said.

"Sorry."

"Irving said that the dead travel from place to place, but not everyone can see them. Only a few of the chosen."

"Of whom he counts himself one."

"Well, he does have a special gift."

"I doubt it was a gift to you. How much did it set you back?"

"Fifteen thousand dollars," she said, lowering her eyes and blushing slightly. I tried not to look alarmed or disgusted. "But I'm going to get it all back because I'm going to marry him."

"What are you talking about? Marry him? What are you talking about?"

"I'm not too old."

"That thought never crossed my mind, Edith. At the lowest moment in your life, you're taken in by some ectoplasmic con man. . . ."

"He's not a con man. Don't you believe that there is a world beyond this one?"

"Not in New Jersey."

"You don't believe then."

"Of course I believe. Otherwise I couldn't teach literature. If this world's all we have, then all the art there is doesn't amount to a hill of beans. But I'll tell you something else, Edith. I also believe that when people die, they remain dead. It's not an Abel Gance movie. The dead don't go around driving automobiles in strange cities. Do they ever get stopped by the police? If so, what happens? Isn't it against the law for the dead to operate moving vehicles?"

"Stop it, Richard! Please!"

I do. I can tell that my jokes are failing. What is a friend to do?

"I've seen him myself!"

"What do you mean you've seen him yourself? Who? Whom?"

"Irving . . . my late husband. Irving and I spent two weeks driving all over New Jersey, and finally we spotted him. I saw him myself."

I feel as if I have been punched in the stomach. "You saw him?" I say weakly. I hate this. I hate every moment of it. An intelligent, charming woman being dragged down through sheer desperation into a dark world, becoming the protégée of some semiliterate con man.

"I saw him." She does not seem ashamed to say it. If it had been me, I would have been too embarrassed. If it had been me.

"You saw him?"

"Yes. Irving and I finally saw him in a shopping mall outside of Trenton. I took this photo myself. With Irving's special camera." She places the photo of someone who looks like her late husband on my desk.

"Did you speak to him? Did he see you?"

"No. You can't speak to them. And they can't speak to you."

"How do you know?"

"Because Irving told me. . . . He said he could bring me to my husband, but all I could do was watch him, be with him, in a sense. But he wouldn't talk to me."

"Why not?"

"Because it would be too painful."

He should have kidney stones. Both of them, I thought, but for Edith's sake I refrained from saying anything. It was getting late. I wanted to finish grading the freshman themes and go home. I opened a drawer in my desk and located a small bottle of aspirin, not that the aspirin would do me any good because I can never get the wad of cotton out of the neck of the bottle.

"If I hired Irving, would he find my father for me?" I asked. It seemed a question courteous enough.

"I'm certain," Edith said, dabbing her eyes. "Do you want me to ask him for you?"

"I'm not sure," I say, replacing the aspirin bottle, its cotton wad intact. "I'm not certain it's worth all the effort, I mean if I can't talk to him, or if he can't talk to me. That's the point of it all, isn't it?"

"Not the only one."

"What's the purpose then?"

"To make certain that someone you love is all right."

"If they're dead, they have to be all right. Unless you believe in hell."

"I do."

"And what proof do we have that this isn't hell?"

"None, I suppose. But you also gain immense satisfaction seeing someone you love, someone you thought you would never see again in this life." She stood up. "Well, I finally told you. Someone. I had to tell someone."

"I'm glad," I lied.

"Me too." She opened her pocketbook and replaced her tissues. She started out of my office, but returned. Framed in the doorway, she looked at me and said: "Irving and I are going to be married in a few weeks. May I invite you to the wedding?"

"Of course," I said. But I had no intention of going. What did he do? Dress up someone to resemble Edith's late husband? And for what? Unless he was going to take the money and run. Perhaps fifteen thousand dollars is not enough. It rarely is. Not when there is so much more at stake.

"If you don't want any more of those readers, could you throw the box away for me? Or leave it somewhere for the others?"

"Of course. But let me walk you to your car."

On the way to the parking lot, we refrained from speaking. But I still had a few questions left. When we reached her Ford, I said: "Tell me something, Edith. If you can see your husband now, can you see the rest of the dead?"

She unlocked the door to her car. "You can only see those people you love," she said, not looking at me, "and only with the help of a guide. I could never see them by myself. You have to see them through the eyes of the chosen."

I nodded. "The chosen."

"Yes, the chosen."

I closed the door for her and waited for her to turn on the engine. I refused to let go of the door handle, to relinquish her to a nightmare existence.

I leaned into the open window. "Edith," I pleaded. "Don't do this."

"Do what?" She was staring straight ahead.

"Throw your life away on some crook. You don't need him. He's taking you for all you're worth."

She bit her lip, but she did not turn her head. She refused to look at me. "It has nothing to do with you, Richard."

"I suppose not," I told her, "except I care about you."

"Then prove it, by trusting me. Trusting my good judgment. I think I know a few things too. I'm not a fool."

"No. You're not a fool. But you're acting foolish. It's not quite the same thing."

"You don't know what those three weeks were like, Richard."

"What three weeks?"

"Those three weeks when I was searching for my husband. Irving and I went from town to town, and we stayed in all the best hotels, and we had wonderful meals, and we danced, and we swam, and we knew we were meant for one another. He's a wonderful passionate man."

Right out of the Kama Sutra, I thought.

"Now let go of the door, Richard. I'm sure you have work to do. You always do."

I relinquished my hold on her. I watched as she drove away. Into a new life.

Vitalogist, I scoff. Sigmund Freud was a Vitalogist, I guess. "Freud's dependency on the mother figure was not restricted to his wife and mother. It was transferred to me, older ones like Breuer, contemporaries like Fliess. . . . But Freud had a fierce pride in his independence and a violent aversion to being the protégé" (Erich Fromm in *Sigmund Freud's Mission*).

Maybe Edith knew what she was doing. I hope so.

Hey, Dad, if you're out there. Hello.

snakes

It was one of those blistering hot days outside Silver City and none of us felt like being under the tent, especially Richie Dee with his Mermaid who, of course, wasn't no mermaid at all, but a real live Pueblo Indian girl he had picked up somewhere, and frequently got pregnant and frequently beat up on when there wasn't much better to do. Believe me, there were lots of days when there wasn't much better to do. We could hear Mermaid shrieking and moaning all the way across New Mexico. Some nights he had to tie her down to keep her from running away.

Those were terrible times then, but I wonder if they are much better now. You'd have to be a philosopher to know such things. In truth, she was just an Indian gal, and so I guess we didn't have to worry about her too much.

Me? I'm Joey De-Chug, a distant relative of the late and not-at-all-lamented Apache Kid. I travel with the freak show as a general factotum. *Factotum.* The Governor who owns everything I sit on got that word for me out of a big book once and I've carried it with me ever since. A word like that can make a man feel special; *drunkard* don't quite cover it.

In truth I'm the guy who counts the freak show money and makes sure no one's holding back. And there were quite a few of us freaks then. Lip the Wolf-man, a good-natured guy, middle-aged, married, but his face was all covered with hair. He looked like a walking wire-brush. His teeth were fanglike, because his first winter with the Flotsam and Jetsam Human Caravan of Unexplicable Marvels, he took to gnawing bones with the Governor's dogs. What was the Governor's right name, I kept asking, but he never told me. *Governor* doesn't quite cover it either.

Still, it was something to see, Lip fighting with the German shepherds for a piece of the ham action. More than once it made me lose my appetite, and it takes a lot to make me lose my appetite, because I've seen things to upset the stomach of a leper and I've eaten things that should have been better left alone. Once, to win a bet, I ate a mess of fried scorpions. Didn't taste as bad as you might think. On the other hand they didn't taste as good as you might like them to.

But let me continue. There was also Dolly and Louella Turpin traveling with us, the sexiest of all the Siamese twins. Good-looking, I thought, and quite moral, because they had, as Lip said, a stick up their ass most of the time. Dolly and Louella were in their early twenties and bogged down in the prophets, singing psalms and selling pictures of themselves.

For one reason or another most pictures of the Turpin twins showed them sitting in a chair with a big fat Bible on their laps.

I guess it was the one possession their parents had given them, and so it had sentimental value, though it is difficult to be sentimental when you spend most of your life packing your bags and traveling by train or wagon from one place to another. Sentiment is for those people who stay put.

Then there was Mirella the Tattooed Lady, who was always after Dolly and Lolly to get tattoos on their private parts (two sets), but they would have nothing to do with it. They would have nothing to do with Mirella either if they could help it. Unfortunately, Mirella sat in a booth next to theirs, and so there were a lot of fights I was called on to break up. To tell you the truth, I would rather have wrestled wild bears than have to break up one of those to-dos. Freaks have a way of fighting something fierce, because so much of their lives depends on their being right because the rest of the world is always pressing on them that they are wrong.

As for Louella (billed as Lolly to make a rhyme) and Dolly, those two (one?) would have gone to church if they could, but they knew that their presence would cause too much of a stir, taking attention away from whoever was preaching. From the preachers I've heard, though, I don't think there is much harm in taking attention away from them. They're all so full of high and mighty, and they look down their noses at the likes of us. That is, if there are any others like us. If there are, may God have pity on them!

And from what I've seen, I don't think there is much harm in taking attention away from most people, but then I guess God didn't make much provision in his world for Siamese twins. As for me, I would have built a special church for them. For them all. A church with real wide aisles.

Actually, I would have done most anything for the Turpin twins, because they kept me up nights wondering what it would be like to be in bed with them. A circus in its own right, I'd imagine. Nothing ever came of my thoughts, but they were a comfort to me in those long, whiskey-stained nights, when I couldn't even bear to look at myself in the mirror. At least my thoughts were one thing the Governor couldn't take away from me. Him with his big words. *Factotum* is as far as I got.

There was also Bob the Alligator-skinned Boy from Arkansas. And Jory MacDougald the Armless-Legless Wonder. Foundra the Fat Lady, all 780 pounds of her. Pip the Zip Head. Oh well, it was just us. The whole spectrum of misfits whose forms graced some of the gaudiest sideshow banners of the Old West. It was a time when parents didn't know what to do with children like that but stick them into a sideshow. Even my own well-meaning hungry-as-vultures parents didn't know what to do with me and I was the most normal one of the lot.

"Hum bum!" somebody cried and I could hear the kids chasing one another up and down the streets of the one-horse town we found ourselves stuck in. Of course, if you are traveling with freaks, no matter where you are, you're stuck. No place you can go, really. You have to stay by yourself and mull over the cards God dealt you. Hardly an ace in the lot.

I want to describe Richie to you, but if you don't care what he looks like, you can just skip over this part and go on to the next. It's all right with me. If there is one thing I have learned in life, I learned a long time ago, a man can't please everybody.

Richie, half Mexican, half Texan, and half mean, was six-feet-two with deep black eyes that did not at all seem normal, as if something was missing. He let his hair grow long and tied it up in a purple bandanna. And he wore genuine rattlesnake boots, the best boots on the lot. That sonuvabitch was the smartest of us all. After all, Richie was the one who thought up the mermaid idea.

What he did was cut a hole in the platform, stick his Indian wife down in the middle of it, then attach the bottom half of a large fish to her back. On hot days, she stunk something awful, but that was part of the realism. And it kept the gawks from coming too close. It also helped that Mermaid spoke no English. That kept her from tipping things off. All she had to do was lean her head on her hand and smile. The fact that she was naked from the waist up helped a lot too, except in some towns where the Governor had to tiptoe around on eggs. If there is another thing I learned in life, I've learned that some things you can get away with and some things you can't.

Anyway, it was that sweltering day when we heard a rumor that Billy the Kid was holed up in a boxcar somewhere nearby. Billy and his whole gang had been caught, and the townspeople were all going to ride down to the railroad station and get Pat Garrett and his deputies to turn Billy and Dave and the other Billy over to them for a good-and-proper hanging. No doubt Garrett and his men weren't going to give the Kid up easily. I knew the Governor had an interest in the goings-on, because I had overheard him talking to Lip and some Mexicans, saying that he'd put up good money for the corpses. It would be good business to have the body of Billy the Kid to show around. It would bring a whole new class of gawks. Not just low-life, but people with real taste. People interested in seeing history up close, not just gawking at Mermaid's breasts.

So Richie and I decided, since there was no reason not to, to help the Governor. The more the merrier I said, though Dolly and Lolly were against the whole venture. Exhibiting live people is one thing; exhibiting dead people is another. They didn't want no part of standing under the same tent with the stinking corpse of Billy the Kid. A stinking fish tail is enough. After all, Mermaid never killed anybody. Aside from the fact that Mermaid was going about half-naked, Lolly and Dolly didn't have much against her. They were probably the only true friends she had. They only had to find out some way to talk to one another. Stuck as they were with each other, the Turpin twins were always hot to talk. I guess that was about the only thing they were hot for. And salvation. And children. Lolly talked a lot about getting married and having children, but there were so many problems involved that I didn't think that was ever going to happen. If there is one thing in life I have learned, it is that there are always more problems involved than you would first imagine.

And so it came to pass, to borrow a phrase, if you will, from Dolly and Lolly's favorite reading material, that Richie and I were standing outside the tent, saddling some horses, when Bob the Alligator-skinned Boy comes running up, calling my name.

"Joey! Joey! Guess what?"

"What?" I said, adjusting the saddle to my horse. Not my horse, really, but I guess you could have guessed that.

"Snakes! We was clearing a space down by the river for the cook tent, and guess what? We uncovered about a thousand snakes. Diamondbacks. I never seen so many of them. You and Richie have got to come with us. We're going to kill about a thousand diamondbacks. It's going to be some kind of a record." He was almost jumping out of his boots, which were specially made because his left foot was twisted something awful.

"What for?" Richie asked, twisting his mouth in that queer way he had of twisting his mouth. He seemed to be sneering at everybody and everything.

"What do you mean what for? What for what?" Bob asked exasperated. His clothes were sticking to his body because of the sweat. Even though his skin is all bumpy and crusty, he sweats a lot. A lot. His brown hair was plastered to the top of his skull just as if he had crawled out of the shower.

"What for to get all excited about killing snakes?"

"For the fun of it for one thing," he said to Richie. "Because it's no good to have snakes around, no matter what. They're poison. And also, we can get the skins and sell them. Did you ever think of that? I bet we can get good money for a thousand rattlesnake skins."

Richie's ears perked up. Richie was almost as interested in making some money as the Governor was. Rumor had it that everything Richie once had he had gambled away. Me? Everything I had the Governor owned—lock, stock, and barrel—but that I already told you.

Richie pulled his rifle out of his saddle holster and walked around the horses. "Come on, Joey, let's go kill us some snakes."

"What about Billy?" I asked. "Billy ain't just going to stand around forever in some boxcar, waiting for us to come to him." The Governor must have given Richie something like five thousand dollars to buy the body with. I thought the Governor should go over to Silver City and conduct the transaction himself, but that was the way the Governor was. He never did anything himself if he could help it.

Richie squinted into the sun. "Yeah. So? If there ain't enough snakes, then we'll just come back and go." He twisted his mouth again. When I stared into that mouth with its pointed teeth, I could understand why he'd have to hobble Mermaid to keep her from running.

"There's enough snakes," Bob said, almost jumping up and down. I had been traveling for a long time, and I don't think I ever saw him so excited. He was bursting at the seams. "Hundreds of 'em. I swear. More. I'm going to get the others."

"Well, get some weapons while you're at it," Richie called after him. "You ain't going to kill no diamondback with your bare hands even if you are the Alligator Boy."

Bob was off and running. Richie turned away from the sun toward me. "Well?" He closed his eyes as if he was thinking. Or anticipating, which I guess is the same thing as thinking.

"Okay," I said, returning to my saddlebags to pull out my Colt. "But the Governor's going to be sore as hell."

"Why?" We started down the slope toward the river. I kept a tight grip on my gun. Maybe other people like snakes, I mean I worked long hours with snake charmers and women with snakes around their necks, but it didn't mean I liked to be around them very much. It just meant that it was a job. That's all. Like being ugly. Being ugly was a big job all right. And a rattlesnake could come at you in just a few seconds. They were quick and they were mean, just like somebody else I could name.

"Because he has his heart set on Billy," I told him, looking over my shoulder to see if the Governor was watching us. The Governor was watching everything.

"Let him bring the Kid back then. And I bet you a silver dollar that no boxcar is going to hold Billy and his gang for long. He'll shoot his way out of there before nightfall." The ground was baked hard. My white shirt was clinging to me too.

"We had better wait for Bob, hadn't we?" I said. "He's the only one who knows where they are." Behind me I could hear the squeals and shouts and mutterings around the gawk tent.

"Hell, if Bobskin can find 'em, anybody can," Richie said, not losing any momentum. Me? I was only the factotum. Just something the Governor made up.

Some days I would just stare at the tents strung out in the middle of nowhere, the yellow flags fluttering, and I would think it was just something fantastic, an imaginary town where no one really lived. We came in the night and we departed in the night, and, except for souvenirs, no one would ever know we had been there—had actually been there amid the buffalo droppings, and the wheat fields, and the sand and the dust, and the wind blowing the sawdust this way and that.

"We better do it fast," I suggested. "Then go for Billy."

Richie laughed. It wasn't a natural laugh. Even in the heat his laugh sent a chill up me. But, whatever I thought about him, I had to admire his gift o' gab. Richie could spiel with the best of them. Up and down and all around he could hold the marks spellbound. Coming as I did from a family where my parents would barely make grunting sounds at me, perhaps because they couldn't stand to look at my face, good spiel was something I would crawl through hell for. Talk was a good substitute for living:

"Ladies and Gentlemen, I have the honor to present the world's only living and surviving mermaid. Every man, woman, and child out there is too intelligent to be fooled, and so I place before your discerning eyes, your well-honed judgments, living and convincing proof that mermaids, contrary to rumor, are still alive upon this planet. For a small separate admission fee, you can satisfy your curiosity to your hearts' content. All the way from the Feejee Islands she comes, with nothing on her but a tail. She's half

woman and half fish, and she's completely helpless out of the water, just as a landlubber like me is completely helpless in it. She speaks, but in no known tongue. Sorry, son, no one under eighteen allowed. . . . I want to tell you folks that never before in the history of mankind have everyday curious people like yourselves been privileged to stand before one of the great wonders of the natural world. All the way back to Homer, people have stood in astonishment just at the thought of mermaids. But now you don't have to imagine. You can see for yourself. Sorry, son, no one under eighteen allowed. This way . . . This way . . ."

"What are you standing there daydreaming about?" Richie snapped at me. "Forget about Billy and concentrate." Ah, if he only knew, but he had worked himself up into a lather because he couldn't locate the snake pit. We followed the riverbed for about a quarter of a mile, then turned around and walked back, not talking to one another. Finally the rest of the tent folk caught up to us, and Alligator Bob took over the lead, moving with unexpected grace, chuckling under his breath and smelling blood. Even Lolly and Dolly had been drawn out of the shade in the anticipation of excitement. The Wolf-man was carrying a pickax, and Madge, his wife, was toting a shovel. Mirella had brought her derringer, which I didn't think would do much good. Everybody else was armed to the teeth, with every kind of killing weapon they could get their hands on. Boards. Sticks. Hammers. Rifles. Zip Head had brought some dynamite sticks, but I didn't want to fool with that. But what can you expect from a pinhead? They're dumb and they don't live long to bother anybody very much.

"I thought you said they was down by the river," Richie said to Bob.

"I said we found them while we were going down by the river. As soon as the Chinese cooks saw them, they took off like greased lightning. The snakes really had them spooked."

When I looked behind me, there must have been about twenty people of all shapes and sizes marching behind us. I began to think it looked like outright war. I could only imagine what the Governor would think seeing all his employees decked out for a killing. Unless he looked down and thought we were all on our way to lynch Billy.

Alligator Bob led us up the side of a small hill by the river and then toward a small hollow in the side of the hill. The pit hollow must have been about twelve feet around and ten to twelve feet deep. The diamondbacks were certainly easy to spot. There were hundreds of them all around, some sunning themselves on rocks, some lying under the rocks. The sight of all those snakes in one place, snakes lying on top of one another, snakes coiled about one another, snakes flat on the earth, eating the dust of the earth, almost all of them practically motionless because of the heat. Through the haze, it could well have been a mirage. But, of course, it wasn't. All of those snakes were as real as anything God had created, including the most ugly of us and the most despised.

Richie fired the first shot and caught a rattler through the head. Then more shots, to stir things up. As the snakes started to crawl away, Madge, the Wolf-man's wife, brought down the blade of her shovel, hard, and cut a diamondback clean in half. And then again and again. Soon her high boots were covered with blood. The rest of us didn't hold back either. Awhooping and ahollering, we waded into the hollow and gave those reptiles everything we had. They couldn't hear us, but they could feel our vibrations all right.

Snakes were all around us and were so confused they started striking at themselves. The only people who held back were Dolly and Lolly who had climbed onto the top of a high flat boulder to get a better view. Maybe they didn't approve of the massacre, but they couldn't take their eyes off it neither. Mermaid too, wearing the disguise she always had to wear whenever she was outside the tent—a wig and a veil—so no one could say they actually saw the Feejee Island Mermaid on two legs, stood apart, shouting at us to stop, until Richie had the sense to walk over to her and knock her to the ground. "Shut up, woman," he shouted at her, giving her a kick in the ribs. "If you can't stand it, go back to the tent and leave us alone. We're entitled to some fun, ain't we?" Mermaid just stayed on the ground, didn't cry, didn't say nothing. Maybe deep down she hoped that the snakes would crawl over her and eat her alive, but whenever the rattlers would start in her direction, Mirella would shoot her derringer and the rest of us would come running. I'd say it took us less than twenty minutes to kill over two hundred diamondbacks, not counting hundreds of tiny baby snakes.

Maybe you think it was ugly, but I say it was gorgeous. Ridding the world of all that poison. We shot, we hacked, and we sliced. We cut the heads off them. We used the lifeless bodies as whips to playfully hit ourselves with. Foundra the Fat Lady was a sight to behold, seated on a rock, draping about thirty dead diamondbacks over her fat arms and around her neck. With great delight, Jory would pick them up in his teeth and deposit them into her lap.

"I am the Queen of the Snakes," Foundra announced, picking up a rattler in each hand and swinging them around, over her head.

Me? I was covered with snake blood, as was everyone else. Our faces, our hands.

We didn't even stop when they were dead. We'd pick up the dead ones and slap them against rocks and tree trunks. Then we changed our minds about the dynamite and we put Pip to work blasting snakes out of the small pits they had retreated to.

Whenever a charge of dynamite would go off, hundreds of snakes would come slithering out and we would go after them with pickaxes and shovels and guns. Pip the Zip Head was about as happy as I had ever seen him.

After about an hour of killing, we decided to add some variety to the feast by going around and biting the heads off them. But, of course, it was no big deal for Lip because his teeth were honed for such carryings-on. It was something to hold the face of a dead rattler close up to your own face, stick it deep into your mouth, and then chomp down on the neck as hard as you could. Even Louella and Dolly got into the act and tried their hands (all three of them) at snake-gnashing. It was something to see the blood spurt up into their faces. And then all over their clothes. Soon they looked just like the rest of us.

"Hey, Joey," Lip said to me, holding his fur face close to mine until I had to turn away because of the hotness of his breath. The foulness too. "Do you see what I see?"

"What?"

"Look!" he said, touching the face of a dead rattler. "No eyelids. These snakes don't have no eyelids."

I looked. Lip was right. No eyelids. I could have said something pretty obvious, but I didn't. I merely nodded my head, and turned away, kicking three or four dead snakes off my boots. Then I looked over to see how Mermaid was doing, and noticed nothing but a bare outline on the ground. She was gone. And so was Richie for that matter. And it hit me in a flash. The Governor's five thousand dollars was gone with him too. No doubt about it. That's probably why the Governor wanted me to ride with Richie in the first place. To keep an eye on things. Just to make certain that everything was on the up and up.

Perhaps I should have warned the Governor in the first place, but, in truth, it was none of my business. Besides, the Governor had to be a whole lot better judge of character than I was.

I now want to tell you what happened afterwards, but I'll be brief about it because I know you have someplace better you would rather be. If there's one thing I've learned in life it's that everybody in creation has someplace else where they want to be.

Two days after the snake killing, we pulled up stakes to move on to a little town called Hurly. (The Governor was big on hitting little towns that nobody ever heard of. I also think he wanted to hang close to the Mexican border just in case Richie decided to make a comeback.) It was in Hurly that a terrible silence overtook us. No one wanted to talk to anyone anymore. Was it anger? I don't think so. We had no reason to be angry with one another. We had reason to be angry with Richie, but Richie was gone. Though, of course, we were mad at Mermaid for her going along with him. Why didn't she just kill him and get it over with? Women, even Indian ones, I don't understand at all.

But something happened. Even the Turpin twins took to going off by themselves, sitting in their wagon, not reading, not talking, not sewing, not doing much of anything.

I know we weren't upset about losing the Mermaid exhibit, because in point of fact, once you know how to do it, anyone can do it, though no one ever came forward to replace Richie and his Indian woman. The Governor, of course, had sent a posse after them, but it was more than likely that the Governor's money would never be recovered. It was a pretty big loss, and it was going to take a long time and a lot of hard work to make it up, though there is one thing I have learned in life— there are some things that never can get made up.

There was also something else about the Mermaid exhibit. It was cleansing in a way to be rid of her. Because there was something disturbing about having a fake amid all us real wonders. At first it didn't bother us. But after a while, even though we were afraid to admit it, it did. For Richie and Mermaid, of course, it worked the other way. Being the one fake in a world of true freaks added to Mermaid's credibility.

After playing Hurly for a day, the Flotsam and Jetsam Human Caravan of Unexplicable Marvels started to unravel. One by one we drifted apart. The Wolf-man was the first to pack up and leave. Though I don't believe it was his idea. Madge had turned sullen and nagging, and poor Lip had no choice. He and his wife weren't getting along, but he followed her. Maybe he figured it was not going to be easy for him to find another woman in his life. Who knows? I never had a woman in my whole life. But Lip went out with a hangdog expression and his face uncombed, not even looking back. It was sad to see them go, and the Governor made no effort to keep them. The Governor, in fact, wasn't speaking to anybody. He was furious with us about the snake killing, and then I think he thought that it would be better to follow Richie's example and just set out fakes. Fakes were easier to deal with. A fake doesn't carry around so much emotional baggage.

Foundra the Fat Lady sat on her chair, fanned herself, and moaned a lot. "That was a terrible thing we did," she'd say over and over. "Why did you make us do it?"

"Do what?" I asked.

"Killing all those innocent snakes. They never did nothing to us." She pulled at her thin skirt. She always dressed quite daintily, though I noticed that the night we came back from the river in Silver City she spent a lot of time burning her clothes. Just a few of her undergarments would be enough to light a prairie by.

"I didn't make you do it," I told her, disgusted with the whole lot of them. "You came of your own free will, because you wanted to get snakeskins like the rest of us."

Pulling her lip, she turned away from me. "No. I didn't take any snakeskins. Not one."

Come to think of it, what Foundra said was true. She didn't skin any snakes. Nobody did. We thought we would go back and have a skinning party, but, for one reason or another, we never did. Never did. Just left the snakes out to dry up in the sun.

"I hate your kind," she said. "Get away from me."

"I hate you too," I told her. I didn't at the time, but I couldn't think of anything better to say. I had no idea what she meant by "my kind" but I wasn't going back to ask her, and she must have meant something and must have spread a lot of poison about me because even Bob gave up speaking to me. Every time I'd walk into the tent, the whole rotten lot of them would just turn away. Not together exactly. Separately, I'd say.

Then outside of Deming, Mirella, who had fallen into a feast of terrible moods, muttering under her breath something about diamonds, wandered off by herself. Didn't even take a suitcase with her. The snake killing wasn't my idea, I told her, but she didn't care one bit. Just wandered off, in the heat of day, muttering. Must have been something for strangers to chance upon a tattooed lady in the middle of the desert. At a distance she looked like an armadillo. More than likely such strangers thought they was seeing a mirage, because they wouldn't know what to think if they didn't have some spieler telling them what to concentrate on. Some days I think my whole life is a mirage.

Two weeks later, on the outskirts of Las Cruces, where we heard rumors regarding human sacrifices, Zip the Pinhead, who had lived longer than any of us expected, crawled off and died. His last words were, "Tell Joey I forgive him." But I had no idea what he was forgiving me for. We gave him a decent burial, and Dolly and Louella sang hymns. They had pure, lyrical, soprano voices, but it was the first time I had heard them say anything in weeks. They spent a lot a time during the days in the bathtub, trying to get themselves clean, I guess. I could have peeked, but I didn't. For some reason I lost my curiosity about them.

I know Alligator Bob would have left, but he really had nowhere else to go. The Governor owned him lock, stock, and barrel too.

As for Billy the Kid—it was just as well that Richie and I didn't take the trouble to try to buy the body, because it turned out there wasn't any body to buy.

Billy, in fact, had found a better place to be, because that night so long ago back in Silver City, we heard that Billy the Kid and his gang had blasted their way out of the boxcar, making good his escape, just the way Richie said he would.

in the
house of
simple
sentences

Sentence number one: *We, in spite of nightmares, still fall asleep.* Variations on that sentence include:

1. In spite of nightmares we fall asleep still.
2. We fall asleep still in spite of nightmares.
3. Still we fall asleep in spite of nightmares.
4. In spite of nightmares, still we fall asleep.

And so forth. I had not fallen asleep, but I could have sworn that the old man sitting across from me had said, "I am God." Yes, he had said it all right.

Out loud. Everybody heard him, and that included four or five women, two men, myself, and Cappy, who owned and worked behind the counter of Cap's Café. The man who had said it was seventy or eighty years old, had a beard, a mane of white hair, a black coat that hung to his ankles, and a ragged pair of pants, capped with a flowered sport shirt. Cappy insisted that the old man was a bum. I, all of eleven at the time, was not so certain.

Two women sipping coffee at the lunch counter didn't look up. They went on drinking, smoking their cigarettes, and talking as if nothing had happened. I sat across from the old man at one of the tables. Every day, after school, I came into Cap's place to sweep up and run errands. Cappy didn't pay much, but it was work. Besides, Cappy was a good guy. Everybody liked him. He had a humped back and he wasn't any taller than I was. He liked to play games, and I was good at checkers and chess. When business was slack, Cappy and I played games, and he tried to tell me about women. I was very interested in women. Even when I was sitting across from the man who said he was God, I tried to listen to what the women were saying.

Sentence number two: *The ocean behind me had turned dark brown, almost black.* The ocean smelled like the coat of Zeus, for Zeus was the old man's name. He repeated it three times and spelled it out, letter by letter, as if there were any other way to spell it, while I wrote it on a napkin. ZEUS.

But what ocean was it? Was it a real ocean? Or was it an ocean that existed only in the mind's geography? I woke up thinking that the ocean was making a terrible pounding sound. I thought how awful for the ocean to turn such an unnatural color. It cannot be a good omen.

Outside the café the Florida sky had also turned black. The sky matched the ocean of my dreams. The old man, clinging to his cup of free coffee, said, "I am the thrower of lightning bolts."

I thought I should ask Zeus: How can you throw the lightning bolts when you are sitting in Cap's Café?

But I did not ask him the question. Instead I told him my dreams. It was a mistake.

The woman at the counter, the one smoking cigarettes with her friend, was named Hilda. She worked at a shop called The Corset Box. She told her friend, "You know there are Jews who actually put flowers on Hitler's grave?"

"I don't believe it," her friend said.

"It's true." The woman blew out smoke rings, and the circles fell into one another.

"I think I had better get back to the shop before it rains," the second woman said.

"I know somebody who actually did it," Hilda insisted. She opened her red pocketbook and searched for some change to leave on the counter.

"Why?"

"They wanted to show how magnanimous they are. I think they're sick. They ought to be shot."

"The whole world is sick," Hilda's friend said. She stood up and pulled at her skirt. Her slip had been showing.

I thought: someday I am going to know more about the world. To dream of a dark and choppy ocean, Zeus said, means that the dreamer needs supreme courage for events that lie ahead.

Yes, I thought, I need courage for the events that lie ahead. Cappy sat in front of the counter and sipped coffee. He was wearing his apron. Otherwise he would have been mistaken for one of the customers. He sat with his back toward Zeus. Cappy had no use for gods. It was God who had given him the hump on his back. Maybe the women loved him all the same, I thought.

The women went outside where it was starting to rain.

"Who's the woman in the red dress?" Zeus asked.

"Hilda," I told him.

"What's her last name?"

"Aronoff."

"I'd like to lay her," Zeus said. He grinned at me. His teeth were very crooked, very yellow. But what did teeth have to do with gods? He didn't look like a god. He looked like a drawing in my first-grade primer. "I didn't mean to shock you," he said.

"You didn't," I lied. I was eleven, but I was a very stupid eleven, even though I was my school's spelling champ. In a few days I was scheduled to go to the county spelling bee. If you won the county and then won the state, you got a free trip to Washington.

Combining sentences we get: *Because I had no courage, the sea behind me had turned dark brown, almost black.*

My father is walking along the beach. He tells me about a woman he knows in a pink trailer. The pink trailer is at the end of the beach. The woman in the pink trailer owns a horse, a black horse. The black horse has slammed my father's right hand against the trailer door and has broken it. It, the hand. My father says, "The horse has broken my hand." He speaks to me as if I were a small child. But this is many years later when I am an old man myself.

Question. Not a sentence. *Who lives in that trailer if it is not my mother?*

When Cap's Café closes at six o'clock, my mother will pick me up to take me home. I want Zeus to leave before then. I do not want Zeus to meet my mother.

Suppose the ocean is life, as it often is. Often it is. Often I could walk down a narrow street between a tight row of white houses. At the end of the street is the ocean. It is dark green. Not brown. Not black. But the ocean smells like the rags of Zeus. Because I have no courage, the ocean is not green. Because I have no courage, the ocean smells foul.

"My wife, Hera, died a long time ago," Zeus says. He pours spoonful after spoonful of sugar in his mug. I do not understand how he can drink anything that sweet.

"If your wife is a goddess how can she die?" Cappy asks, but Cappy does not turn around to ask his question. He sits with his back to the god.

"Gods die," Zeus insists. "Gods die all the time. I died a couple of times myself, when people forgot all about me. But I've got staying power. I live on another planet and only every once in a while I return to Earth. I like walking the earth, going to and fro upon it. Everything about the earth—its oceans, its mountains, its animals—reminds me who I am. You, son, are fortunate. You can grow and change. Gods cannot grow, gods cannot change. I always am whatever I was. But you can become something else. And you will."

"Pop, drink your coffee and go," Cappy says, still not looking at the man. Cappy is in his late forties, about as old as my father, and he has seen a lot of characters come and go. Cappy himself is a character, but I never once heard him claim that he was a god.

"How do I know you're a god?" I ask the man, staring into his clear-blue eyes. Everything about Zeus is old, except his eyes.

"You don't want me to prove that, son," Zeus says.

"Why not?"

"Because it means somebody has to die."

"If you are a god," I ask him, watching the storm through the plate-glass window, "can you go anywhere you wish to go?"

Zeus shakes his head.

"Why not?"

"Because I have my own destiny to contend with. I can control anything, but I cannot control the Fates."

I don't know what the old man is talking about, but I don't ask him. I want him to go away.

"Jesus," Cappy says. "Why don't you get out of here before I call the cops." I know what's bothering Cappy. People like Zeus drive away customers. But nobody's going to come out in the rain.

"It's pouring out," Zeus says. He thrusts his cup and saucer in my direction and winks. He wants a refill. I go get him a refill. Cappy looks at me with hatred.

"It's raining," I tell him.

"Everybody's got an excuse," Cappy says. "Especially God. He's got the most excuses of all."

When I bring Zeus the cup of coffee, he says: "Beware of scorpions. Florida's filled with scorpions, isn't it."

"Some parts of it are, I guess."

"That woman Hilda is as beautiful as a swan," Zeus says. "I think I'll go look her up."

"Why don't you do that," Cappy says. "See if she gives you the time of day."

I know something that Zeus doesn't. Cappy's got a crush on Hilda himself, but he doesn't have the nerve to do anything about it. Hilda's pretty down-to-earth and she always has a snappy answer.

I think: if he's a god, why doesn't he fly? Why doesn't he float in the air, surrounded by flames? If he is Zeus, as he claims, why does he sit at a small table in Cap's Café, hunched over a white mug of coffee like an old man waiting to die? Finally he stands up and leaves. He walks out into the rain as if it is nothing at all. Good riddance to bad rubbish, Cappy says. He doesn't really mean it, but he says it anyway. It makes him feel good.

I live in the house of simple sentences. Nobody at home talks much, so I don't tell them about Zeus. My parents wouldn't know what to make of it. I feel that religion should change with the times. My father feels that religion should never change. If it is the Truth, how can it change? We have terrible shouting arguments about it. It is the Greek style. We have a lot of feelings, but we do not know what to do with them.

Every Saturday morning at Cap's Café, the cops—at least the three who ride the horses through the main street of town—drop in for free breakfast. I finally understand why I get paid so little for my work. Cap gives everything away. Actually, I am underage. Cap has to pretend that I really am not working for him. Everybody else, however, knows the truth. Even the cops.

One is a lieutenant. The other two men don't have any stripes. They are young, and the youngest of the three is a blonde-haired man named Honninger. When the three patrolmen sit down, their gun holsters hang over the sides of the tiny red stools. Their guns, their handcuffs, the bullets in the wide belts, their brown leather jackets—it all speaks of authority.

"Who is that old guy who goes around claiming he's God?" Honninger asks. I don't get to answer, because Cappy, clapping platters down on the yellow formica counter, tells him: "Arrest the old geezer the next time you see him. It's for his own good. He's as looney as they come. He's not playing with a full deck. He ought to be up in Chattahoochee with the rest of the clowns. It's for his own good." I figured that out myself, he tells me. "The reason God came to Florida is not because he needs a vacation, but because he wants to be close to Chattahoochee."

Chattahoochee is where they send the insane. My parents and I had passed the place a couple of times during our drives across the state. The people inside the asylum wear straitjackets and talk in sentences nobody understands. It's a standing joke in all the families in Florida.

Honninger's left hand is thickly bandaged. He cut himself disarming a robber. "Funny thing about that old geezer," he says. "I saw his picture in the paper a few weeks back. I could swear he's the same guy in that three-car pileup on U.S. 1. When they rushed him to the hospital he was DOA."

"What's DOA?" I ask.

"Dead on Arrival. Like these eggs," the lieutenant says. He laughs at his own joke.

"Well, he's not dead now," Cappy says, sliding the ketchup bottles down to me. I stack them up by twos, mouth to mouth, so that the blood from one can run into the other. "He comes in here every night like clockwork, freeloads a meal, fills the kid's head with wild stories. He ought to be run out of town. It's for his own good."

"He doesn't come in here every night," I tell Cappy. "It's only every once in a while."

"Well, you're not the one buying him coffee, are you?" Cappy says. He smears the grill with cooking oil. Some days I wonder if I smell like onions myself. "Anyway he's costing me customers."

"You don't have customers," the lieutenant says, laughing. "All you have is people that come in here and eat. Only places that have tablecloths can claim customers."

"Maybe the old guy had a twin brother," Honninger adds. "Maybe it was his twin brother that was killed in the crash and maybe that's what drove him wacko."

"Maybe you ought to take up psychology," the third cop says. His name is Bill. I know all the cops in town. There aren't that many. I also have learned that the gods have brothers. Are brothers. Hades lives under the earth. Poseidon is god of the sea. But is it a real sea, or only a sea of the imagination? A tiny sea found at the end of a narrow lane.

"It's got to be his twin brother," Honninger insists. "Or else he died and came back to life."

"And maybe there are little green men on Mars," Bill says.

"The paper says another UFO has been sighted," Cappy says.

"Always a UFO sighting," the lieutenant sighs. "That's all the calls we get these days. I tell you the whole state is going off the deep end."

On Saturdays I put in a full eight-hour day. When I get off work, I see Zeus walking down the street with Hilda on his arm. It's weird, I think. But I won't tell Cappy. Cappy's feelings would be hurt.

Maybe it's a way of proving to me that he's a god.

More sentences. The blood of one runs into the other. The wind is blowing the branches aside so that the moonlight can reach us. He would be hurt. He claims to be the captain of a ship. Hence, Cappy.

* * *

Sentenced. A person is brought before the gods and is sentenced to live. But who sentenced the gods to live? That is the unaskable question. Many years later I dream that I am walking along the ocean at night. Out on the ocean is a series of screens. Motion picture screens. War movies are being shown. And science fiction films. Images are landing from another planet and the tide is washing them in and out. Unidentified Flying Objects. And the waves are white. The sea beyond is black. Scorpion-black. A light shone on the darkness.

It is the week before Christmas. In Florida, Christmas does not stand out the way it does in the North where there is the possibility of snow. In the Catholic church, my mother and my sisters are listening to the priest read from the Gospel of John:

> In the beginning was the Word, and the Word was with God, and the Word was God. The same was in the beginning with God. All things were made by him; and without him was not any thing made that was made. In him was life; and the life was the light of men. And the light shineth in darkness; and the darkness comprehended it not.

I have stayed home with my father, for we are cleaning out the garage. When he leans over to pick up a rake from under a wheelbarrow, a scorpion scurries forth and stings my father on the thumb. My father, taken by surprise, straightens up, gives a cry of pain or surprise, a gift to the unknown, and leaps back. I watch the scorpion run down the rake handle, then onto the dirt floor. My father picks up a shovel and goes after it, pounding the insect into the ground. I tell my father to call the doctor, but I know what my father is thinking. Doctors cost money. He continues to clean out the garage as if nothing has happened. I watch his thumb swell.

When we go inside the house, my father takes a razor blade, cuts an X on his thumb, and sucks out the poison. But he's not feeling well. So he lies down to sleep.

I must find Zeus before it is too late.

1. I must find Zeus.
2. You must find Zeus.
3. We must find Zeus.
4. See Zeus change into a swan.
5. See Zeus carry away innocent victims.
6. Run, Jodie, run.
7. In the beginning was the Word and the Word was God.
8. See God.
9. See God die.

At the Catholic church, the Church of the Little Flower (was there anywhere in the world the Church of the Big Flower? the Huge Flower?), there is only the choir rehearsing for its program of Christmas music. I love the smell of a church. The smell of candle wax. The smell of the Holy Water. The stained-glass windows that comprehend the light. The choir singing:

> O Magnum mysterium et admirabile
> sacramentum, ut animalia viderent
> Dominum natum, jacentem in presepio.
> O beata Virgo, cujus viscera meruerunt
> portare Dominum, Jesum Christum.
> Alleluia.

If God speaks to us, He speaks to us in dead tongues. I run into the church and I run out. I am looking for the wrong god in the wrong place. Even I know that, but I have the presence of mind to call Hilda. Hilda Aronoff. When she answers the phone, I tell her who I am and I ask if she can tell me where Zeus is.

"Try the park," she says. "That's where he usually sleeps it off."

And off I go to the tiny park with its bandshell and sundial. The sunlight falls across the flowers in such a way that it becomes Time. Is Time. The park is deserted. I am running through a world in which no one lives except when memory brings them alive. Even the policemen on horseback are nowhere to be found. Nothing is to be found but the light falling across the hibiscus. And at home, if my father is dreaming, what is he dreaming? *O Magnum mysterium.*

In front of the tiny bandshell, where soon people will be gathering to sing Christmas carols,

> O come, all ye faithful,
> Joyful and triumphant,
> O come ye, O come ye to Bethlehem.
> Come and behold Him,
> Born the King of Angels:
> O come, let us adore Him,
> O come, let us adore Him,
> O come, let us adore Him,
> Christ, the Lord

are row after row of green wooden benches, and there in the very back lies the old man asleep, his grizzled face toward heaven. Come and behold Him. And the stench about him. And the flies crawling down his coat. I shake him. I shake him hard. "Mr. Zeus, wake up." But he will not wake. I pound on his chest with my fists. But nothing will open those eyes. There is a dried river of blood at the corner of his mouth. And in his hands is nothing.

"The scorpions. You warned me about the scorpions!" I cry. "You must do something."

I look at his hands. How swollen they are. How swollen his entire life has been.

And from the church, the bells are ringing their old familiar carols.

What can any of us do, when the gods need as much help as we do?

Running back through town, I finally locate my friend Honninger. Honninger is flirting with a teenaged girl in front of the movie theater, and so he is not pleased to see me.

"Zeus is dead," I tell him. "He's in the park, near the band-shell, and he's dead."

"No, Jodie, he's not dead. He's just drunk."

"I tried to wake him up."

"Dead drunk."

"No," I tell him. "I know the difference. He wasn't breathing. There was blood coming out of the side of his mouth."

"For Christ's sake," Honninger says, holding his hands up to the sky. "That bum is more trouble than he's worth." The teenaged girl looks on with admiration, confusion, and fear. I want to fall in love. I want to tell her, Hey, I'm the spelling champ.

"All right, Kid," Honninger tells me. "I'll take care of it. It's nothing for you to worry about."

"I'll go with you," I tell him.

"No, you go home. It's nothing for you to get involved with." He mounts his horse. The sound of the heavy hooves on the road fills my heart with wonder.

At home, the house is filled with tragedy. Everyone is seated around the kitchen table and my mother's eyes are all teary. My grandmother has died. My father's mother. In the morning, my father must fly to Boston.

My father insists on going through a ninth-grade spelling book, and so we sit outside the house, sit in the front yard, where he calls out the words to me. There is very little light. I wonder how he sees. What is going through his mind with his mother dead? All those words waiting to be placed into sentences:

Extract	Verbatim
Carrion	Intrigue
Bereaved	Fossil
Dynamo	

Letter by letter they are spelled. Word by word, sentence by sentence, we form our lives and speak our tenderness. Dreams we have, but they are not large enough. Perhaps they are large, but we are not large enough.

Is it possible to use all the above words in a single sentence?

From the dynamo, I, bereaved, say verbatim I shall stoop to intrigue in order to extract fossil carrion. Impossible? Perhaps. No doubt nonsense.

My father looks up from the spelling book and sees a strange light orbiting far off. It is not a star. It is not a planet. It is not a plane. My father points it out to me and we sit and study it for nearly twenty minutes. Long enough for me to get goose bumps.

"There's something funny about that light," my father suggests. My heart is in my throat and I begin to tremble. Perhaps I am just exhausted.

My life is an Unidentified Flying Object. I am looking at something in the sky, something very strange, something beyond our planet. It is my father's mental state objectified. He suggests that we go inside to call the police. I am terrified. My six-year-old sister is in the living room. She is howling with terror. She is hysterical. The thought of visitors from another planet is overwhelming. I cannot bring myself to go outside to look at the sky, with its strange whirrings.

When my father gets off the phone, he says: "I'm not the first to report it. They said that they got fifteen or twenty calls already. The air force is going to send up a plane to investigate." He pauses, and takes my sister into his arms.

"By the way," he says. "Honninger said for me to tell you not to send him on any more wild-goose chases."

"What goose chase?"

"I don't know. He just said it wasn't funny. You sent him to look for somebody who wasn't there."

"Wasn't there?"

"I'm just telling you what he said."

I do not understand and take my misunderstanding into another room, as I take them now into another life, where we, in spite of nightmares, still fall asleep.

laces

Walking up the Plockenstrasse, Joseph, dressed in robes and sandals, his head shaved, his arms dripping with bracelets, overheard two young college students arguing over the virtues of brass knuckles and the vices of knives.

It's not that the facts were not always wrong, it's just that the facts were always there. The facts were the facts. One fact was this: Joseph Harranger was going home. Other facts had to do with *Die Katastrophe,* and the death of his father, the old scholar, the man once up to his ears in Sanskrit, he who devoted so much of his academic life to Mayura.

"I'd rather have brass knuckles than a knife," one man said.

"Me too." The second exhibited a great need to agree. His round, tanned face lit up with agreement. "I mean a knife . . ." and then the conversation trailed off.

Joseph laughed. He hadn't heard a good academic discussion in months. The note he carried in his left hand said simply: Father dead. Joseph's brother had written it and had stuffed it in Joseph's mailbox. Father dead. Elgart hadn't even the grace to call him. No doubt he hadn't even delivered the message himself. He probably had one of the bank's messengers do the dirty work for him. 11:23 P.M. What a shock it had been to open the mailbox and find a slip of white notepaper and a hastily scrawled note in a handwriting that was no longer familiar. Bank letterhead, no less. Not even the simplest personal touch, as if any personal touches were left.

The street was littered with newspapers proclaiming fresh disasters. Some personal. Some international. What interested Joseph most of all was how human beings, animals, and plants knew things. So much knowledge in the world, each person bearing within himself or herself different versions of events called history or news or gossip. Or perhaps destiny.

Sometimes the knowledge was brought home by newspaper headlines:

Die Katastrophe

Am Donnerstagabend—nach amerikanischer Ziet—sagte der Funk die knappe Meldung von dem furchtbaren Unglück in die Welt hinaus. Bald überstürzten sich die Nachrichten und gaben, zum Teil in den einzelheiten sich widersprechend, ein Bild von dem Hergang der Katastrophe. Aus der Fülle der Schilderungen läßt sich folgendes Gesamtbild herausschälen:

Sometimes by notes stuffed into mailboxes. Sometimes by meditation. Oftentimes by dreams. HINDENBURG EXPLODES.

33 KILLED. 65 SURVIVORS. Lakehurst, New Jersey. One could wish it was merely an ugly dream.

"What are you doing here?" Elgart demanded, dressed as he was in black, standing in the doorway to the family house on Goethe Street, his six-foot-two-inch frame blocking the entrance of any intruder. Elgart was forty-five, some three years older than Joseph. A banker whose gray hairs, whose Prussian bearing, whose stiffened stance, whose formal dress, betokened a person of importance. Of great importance. Too important to be anybody's brother.

"He's my father too," Joseph said.

"Is he? Was?" Elgart removed a white handkerchief from his coat pocket and lifted it to his nose as if warding off an unfamiliar scent. His blue eyes were watery. "You meant nothing to him and he meant nothing to you. And now that he is dead, you come. To a house where you are not wanted."

Nothing Elgart said could surprise his younger brother. Joseph did not even regard the words as insulting. They were merely words coming from a foreign source, words needing no translation. Elgart, for all Joseph cared, might as well have been somewhere in New Jersey, wherever New Jersey was. They both had been young children when their mother had died. They had been very little comfort for one another then.

Joseph looked past Elgart into the long and darkened hallway where the small mahogany table, one of the Harranger family's heirlooms, bore the cards of condolences, the stacks of newspapers, both German and English, the official bank letters, and saw Elizabeth, Elgart's young and black-haired wife, gliding with astonishing attractiveness toward them.

"Do you prefer brass knuckles or knives?" Joseph asked.

"What? What are you talking about, you oaf?" Elgart barked. An elegant seal in a seal's elegant dress, Joseph thought. Perhaps they weren't brothers. Perhaps his father had committed some youthful indiscretion. "Get away from the door. Go home. Are you threatening me? I have Schutzstaffel in there. They'll do anything I ask them. Anything."

"I'm coming in and you can't stop me," Joseph said.

Elizabeth, standing as tall as her husband, in a long black-velvet gown, leaned lightly on her husband's right shoulder. "Please, Elgart. It would be wrong for us to keep him away. Our guests will all comment on it."

"They'll talk anyway. Look at the way he dresses. Is this proper dress for a mourner? He dresses like a girl. Like a poof."

"I am a poof," Joseph said simply. He kept his gaze on his brother's young wife. She had once been an actress. What could she have seen in such a pretentious seal? And to have children by him? Just to contemplate the act with a man like Elgart should bring on waves of nausea.

"First we take care of the Jewish problem and then persons like you," Elgart said, mustering as much dignity as he could.

"Give me five minutes and I'll go," Joseph said to Elizabeth. "I won't cause any problems. Promise."

"You don't cause problems, you are a problem." Elgart wiped his nose and shook his head, but he allowed his wife to take his arm and lead him away from the door. "Five minutes, then out!" he shouted.

Elgart had been right. As usual. The parlor and dining areas were crowded with men in uniforms. The men in dark suits were no doubt Elgart's banking friends.

"Where is Goering?"

"At the Creative People's Fair."

"Ah!"

A tall plump man with white hair laughed. "I never trust any project that has the word *creative* attached to it." The others joined in. Elgart gritted his teeth.

The sofas and chairs were crammed with plump women and children. Joseph's nieces and nephews were crowded off into a corner, with Hilda, the youngest, age five, weeping and not knowing what to make of the fuss. No doubt Hilda had arrived into their lives unplanned, although Joseph could not imagine Elgart leaving anything to chance, most especially his sperm.

The house had remained very much the same since Joseph had abandoned it so many decades before. The rich smells of the heavy furniture and deep carpets crept over him. The chandelier burning, the piano, the bright white buttons to push for electricity.

"Where?" he asked.

"In there," Elizabeth said, indicating a small room annexed to the parlor. He could make out the casket and the flowers and the candles. The night before he had dreamt of his father. He had visited him in this very house and had taken him in his arms and had said all the words he had been ashamed to say before. Now it was too late, since there would be no father to hear them. Death was terrible, but not for the reasons people thought. It was terrible because it only brought out the cliché in everyone. Everything that was trite and worn. Nothing in the human heart could rise above the occasion, unless one could speak, not the language of the living, but the language of the dead.

The uniforms turned and stared. Elgart, in embarrassment, beat a slow retreat toward the liquor cabinet. Brandy too had a soul.

"I'm very sorry," Elizabeth said.

Did she mean it, Joseph wondered. "I want to be alone with him."

"I understand." Elizabeth entered and whispered some words to a few of the mourners, who nodded and bowed and exited, hardly daring to look at the intruder.

"The last radio message," one of the officers said, "was a salute to lost zeppelins."

"Ah yes, the Hamburg Naval League."

"Weren't you a friend of Walter Bernholktzer?"

The officer nodded. "Died."

"We managed to hang a temporary curtain," Elizabeth told Joseph, "but I'm afraid it's not thick enough. It doesn't keep the noises out, but it will give you some privacy. Elgart wanted to be alone with the casket too." When everybody had emptied the foyer, Joseph entered. Behind him, Elizabeth drew a dark-red curtain.

"The *Hindenburg* was insured for over two million dollars," an SS officer said to Elgart. "Were you aware of that?"

"Yes." Elgart nodded and, looking toward the closing curtain, frowned. "I was aware of that."

The old scholar in the wooden casket was at peace with the world and himself. But his face looked waxed. The tip of a white and scented handkerchief peeked out of his coat pocket like a small banner of surrender. His hands, liver-spotted and freckled, were folded over his stomach. Nothing about death resembled sleep. Nothing. And nothing more to do now but to perform the miracle of resurrection, as it came to Joseph in a dream.

Joseph kissed the tips of his own fingers and pressed them to the old man's forehead. Behind him and outside the curtain he could hear laughter. He bowed his head, folded his own hands, and started to recite:

jambharatibhakumbod iva dadhatah sandrasindurarenum
raktah sikta ivaughair udayagiritatidhatudharadravasya
ayantya tulyakalam kamalavanaruceva runa vo vibhutyai
bhuyasur bhasayanto bhuvanam abhinava bhanavo
bhanaviyah

A dead language for a dead man. His father would have appreciated that. If one could not be ironic standing in front of a corpse, then where would irony ever thrive?

bhaktiprahavaya datum mukulaputakutikotarakrodalinam
laksmim akrastukama iva kamalavanodghatanam kurvate ye
kalakarandhakarananapatitajagatsadhvasadhvamsakalyah
kalyanam vah kriyasuh kisalayarucayas te kara bhaskarasya

Onward and downward through stanza after stanza of *The Suryasataka of Mayura,* until the entire room took on the glow of unearthliness and a silence so silent that Joseph could hear

Elgart's wife talking, discussing the Prussian Theatre of Youth, in the other room. It was eerie. The voices didn't belong here. But perhaps Claudius wanted to hear what was happening in rooms other than the one he was in.

Joseph, with head still bowed, chuckled to himself. He had not heard a scholarly discussion in months. His father, now floating free of the casket, nodded.

"It's obvious why they chose to present *Henry IV,*" Elizabeth was saying. "It's a parable for all of our German youth. For sixteen years now, Germany has done nothing but swill beer like Falstaff and now along comes young Henry. He will eventually—like the Hilter Youth—find his way to his rightful throne, the divinely appointed leadership."

"I see what you mean," a man said.

"You memorized it all," Joseph's father said, his face glowing with amazement. "All of it?" So much younger he looked. A young man's face.

"Much of it."

His father had no shoes. He was in his stocking feet. No sense in wasting good shoes underground, for where would the old man walk to? How wonderful to be dead. No more shoelaces to tie. He doesn't tie his shoelaces anymore. Who said that? It was a euphemism, a calm way to say a man had died.

"You do?"

"Yes," the man said to Elgart's wife. "The divine right of kings, as Shakespeare understood it, an idea that has descended directly from ancient Egypt when the pharaoh was actually a god on earth. Today we simply translate that notion to the divine rights of leaders."

"Our Fuehrer would approve."

"It was for him that such a production was conceived."

"I've read what some of the critics have written about it: 'The fight of a father for the heart of his son,' which means 'the fight of Adolf Hitler for the heart of German youth.'"

"We shall keep translating Shakespeare," said Elizabeth, "until we get it right."

"What are you speaking?" Hilda asked.

Joseph stopped reciting and turned to face his brother's youngest daughter. He had not been aware that she had been watching him.

"Hello," Joseph said, turning away from his father's spirit dissolving into air, into thin air. Had his father desired so much the discussion of *Henry IV* that he had lifted the words into his hands and had transported them, syllable by syllable, toward the chamber of the casket? He was so fond of Shakespeare. All the old lovely words had vanished. "I haven't seen you in a long time."

"Are you my uncle?" Hilda asked. She cautiously came forward and peered into the empty coffin. How like his brother to have his children face up to harsh realities early on.

"I suppose I am."

"My mother says you are."

"Of course I am your uncle. We just don't see very much of one another."

"What have you done to Grandpa?"

"Nothing."

"Why isn't he here?"

Joseph removed his wire-frame glasses, pinched his nose, and shook his head. "I have no control over these things."

"Did Grandpa go to heaven?"

By way of an answer, Joseph's shoulders shook and he started to sob.

"Yes," Joseph said, finally. The room was flooded with a golden aura. Hilda's yellow hair and dark-blue dress were haloed. The laces of her left black shoe had come undone.

"I want to go to heaven too," Hilda said.

"You don't want to go to heaven so soon," Joseph said. He knelt down on the heavy carpet to help his niece with her shoelaces. "Can you tie your own shoelaces?"

"Sometimes," she said.

"But not now."

"Not now. Can you teach me?"

"No."

"Why not?"

The curtain dividing the room of mourning from the living room was being pushed to one side.

"Because it would be easier to teach you to fly than it would be to teach you how to tie shoelaces. Teaching a child to tie her shoelaces is one of the more difficult of all human tasks."

Elgart was standing with a member of the SS. The officer said, "Our air minister says the explosion was an act of God."

"Yes, yes," Elgart agreed. "'A higher power, in a few seconds, destroyed what human hands by infinite care had constructed.' I read about it in the papers too."

"That's why I wear sandals," Joseph said. "See? Then I don't have to worry about laces. I don't tie my shoelaces anymore." What was it that Alfred Groeinger, the twenty-year-old chef on the *Hindenburg,* had said, just as he closed his eyes and just as the blazing zeppelin sank to earth? "I jumped—and I am alive!" And so Joseph, who had once met the Groeinger family in this very same house, repeated Alfred's words but in another tense. "I jump and I am alive!"

"Have you had enough time?" Elgart asked.

Elgart entered the room and lifted Hilda into his arms, as if proving to Joseph that he was indeed a loving father, one who took the responsibilities of child rearing seriously, and who would not deprive even his youngest of the right to mourn. "There are others who wish to pay their respects," he said.

"Uncle Joseph tied my shoelaces for me," Hilda announced, her face brightening.

"Yes, yes," said Elgart, carrying his daughter away from the casket, away from Joseph. "He was always very good at tying things."

As he set her down outside the foyer, Hilda exclaimed, "Grandpa's gone to heaven!"

"We hope so." Elgart scanned the crowd, looking for his wife. He should not have listened to her, followed her advice. If Joseph had sincerely wished to pay his respects to the dead, he could have gone on his own, after everyone had left, to the cemetery and laid a wreath of flowers at the grave. To come to the house like this, dressed in a weird costume, showed no respect. No respect at all.

"Our ambassador says it's sabotage."

"On or off the record?"

"I mean he's not in the coffin anymore. He's gone," Hilda insisted, clutching at her father's leg.

"Shhh. No time for foolishness." Elgart was impatient, wanting his brother to leave.

"Go see!"

Elgart harumphed and crossed to his brother, placing his thick hand roughly on Joseph's shoulder. "Stand up. Stand up," he ordered. "Time to go. You gave your word. No more scenes."

Three members of the Schutzstaffel entered, their heads bared. They marched stiffly toward the coffin. "What is this? An empty casket?" one asked.

"What? What are you talking about?"

Joseph rose and started to back out of the room, his palms pressed together in prayer, his head bowed in meditation.

"What is going on?" Elgart thundered, his face turning red. His heart pounded. He turned from the empty coffin to face his brother. "What have you done with Father? What did you do with the body? No one gave you permission to touch the body! Did you move the body?"

All conversation in the house halted. A seventeen-year-old blonde servant named Olga dropped a silver tray. She covered her face with her hands. Small uncrusted sandwiches littered the carpet.

"Answer me, you clown!" Elgart roared, reaching out to grab Joseph by the shoulders. "What did you do with Father's body?" Joseph stepped backward, out of reach.

Hilda, sitting on the sofa with her brothers, started to cry. Elizabeth released the arm of one of her seventy-year-old maiden aunts and, followed by the other mourners, rushed to her husband's side.

"Elgart, Elgart. Keep calm! What's wrong?"

One of the SS officers stepped between the brothers. Joseph turned, pushed against the crowd, attempting to exit, but the sea of bodies held firm. Men, women, and children craned their necks to get a glimpse of the commotion.

"Elgart, he couldn't have done anything with the body," the young officer said. "We were all here. What could he have done with it? Where could he have put it?"

"Search the room! Search the room!" Elgart commanded, flailing away at the air.

"What's wrong?" the guests whispered among themselves. "The body. The body is missing."

"Missing?"

Elgart broke through a forest of arms, raised his own arm, and slapped his brother hard across the face. Joseph's glasses were knocked from his nose and dangled precariously from his right ear.

"Elgart!" Elizabeth cried. Her face pleaded for help.

"You clown! You clown!" Elgart shouted at his brother. "You come here and ruin everything. I was right in not wanting you to come in."

"I didn't do anything," Joseph said, wiping his eyes. Elgart roughly pushed him away. "Whatever happened, happened," Joseph explained. "I thought Nazis were enamored of mysticism. Are you not going all over the globe searching for the holy grail? The spear that lanced the side of Christ? Our father rose up and went to heaven. What is there to be so upset about? Fall to your knees and be thankful."

"Claudius? What has happened to Claudius?" Elizabeth's old aunt inquired to the moustached banker standing next to her.

"It's very strange," he said. "It's all very strange."

"You pig!" Elgart spat into his brother's face. "You come here and cause such havoc!"

"I don't understand," the aunt said, shaking her head.

Elgart turned to the young officer. "Get him out of here. I don't want him ever to set foot in this house again." The young officer, his face round and leathery, looked at Elgart quizzically but took no offense.

"Hilda! Hilda! Come here!" Hearing her father's anger, little Hilda trembled and did not move. The crowd turned to face her.

"Let Uncle Joseph stay," she whimpered. "He didn't do anything bad."

"Leave her alone," Elizabeth insisted. "What does she have to do with this?"

"Poor child," the aunt said sympathetically. The servants and guests were looking behind curtains, behind furniture, were scampering from room to room in panic.

"She saw everything," Elgart said. "She must have seen him do something." The mourners, frantic with confusion, moved apart, allowing the three members of the Schutzstaffel to take Joseph outside. Elgart crossed to his daughter and knelt down in front of her. He took her shoe in his hand to retie her laces. "Everything's all right, honey. Just tell us what you saw. Did Uncle Joseph take Grandfather out of the coffin?"

Hilda, studying her shoelaces, shook her head.

"What happened?" Elgart demanded. "Certainly you must have seen something. People just don't disappear in midair."

"Oh leave the child alone," Elizabeth insisted. "She doesn't understand."

"Understand?" asked Elgart. "Does anyone here understand?"

"He was in midair surrounded by flames," Hilda answered, her eyes round, her words hardly above a whisper.

"Flames?" Elgart stood up and threw his hands into the air. "What are you talking about?"

"He spoke in a strange language and grandfather just floated out of the coffin. High up and through the ceiling and out of the house." Frightened, her older brother Osmand began to giggle.

"Are you making fun of me? Take her upstairs," Elgart ordered the young servant.

"I'm sorry about the sandwiches," the servant said. Her face was flushed.

"Forget about the sandwiches!" Elgart bellowed. "You think I care about sandwiches! Just take Hilda upstairs before she loses her mind altogether."

"Come Hilda, come," the servant said, holding out her hand.

"And put some other shoes on her. I'm sick of seeing her laces untied all the time!"

"She was thinking about the *Hindenburg*," Elizabeth's theater friend suggested. "That's what got her all confused."

"We can't find Claudius's body anywhere," Herbert, one of Elgart's banker friends, said. "We've looked everywhere."

"It's impossible."

Elizabeth took one of her sons in her arms and paced back and forth, sighing.

"Everybody go home! Go home!" Elgart commanded. "Go home! Go home!" His head throbbed.

"This is terrible," Elizabeth's aunt said. She clucked her tongue apprehensively. "The worst thing that has ever happened to us."

"Mass hypnosis! That's what it has to be!" Elgart sank to the sofa. He pounded his fist into his hand until his hand ached. "I should never have let him come in here. Never. Never."

Herbert sat beside his friend. "The SS will take care of him. You have no fear on that score. There are some things we cannot tolerate."

"This is terrible," Elizabeth's aunt repeated, shaking her head. She gripped her cane and walked back and forth. Someone had turned on the radio to get the latest update on the *Hindenburg*. "The worst thing that has ever happened to us."

the
house
wherein
i dwell

Howard's agent had warned him: This
year no one was hiring hysterical writers. But Howard was not hysterical. He
was merely out of work.

Dear Sirs:

This is to inform you that the
Death's Head Moth takes its
name from the fact that on its
thorax there are markings that
form the shape of a human skull.
I should also like to point out to
you that, in 1945, one out of two
American families owned telephones. Well, not owned them
exactly. At least, one out of two
Americans had telephones inside

their home where they got up in the morning and worried how to pay the rent, how to carry the mortgage another month, how to drag themselves to a job where the boss treated them with complete indifference.

I thank you for your interest in this matter. If, however, you should be actively seeking a television script for your forthcoming series on famous blowjobs, etc. etc.

I remain your humble servant, etc. etc.

Etc.

And a very big ETC. it was. Howard's wife was expecting twins. Maybe triplets. Why not go for quintuplets? A sextet? More lives stalking in and out of the cupboards of municipal housing. More lives on the way and the money running out.

Money was always running out. It had nowhere else to go. As soon as he thought he had some *dinero,* some dollar bills safely locked up in a closet somewhere, the bills and coins and unbounced checks changed miraculously into moths (moths with human skulls) and ate up the children's clothing, and the mother's clothing, and the father's clothing, ate up the fabric of entire beings, chewed their way through shoes and socks, devoured the paper-thin closet door, and made their hysterical bid for freedom, complete freedom, complete artistic freedom, and, throwing a wet, but sterile, kiss good-bye on the way out, flew a brief and immaculate journey to the banker, the baker, and the candlestick maker.

News filtered fitfully over the wires. The bones of the dead to be moved. How could one tell the living from the dead? Because the living had creditors. The dead had no creditors. Death was just another way of declaring bankruptcy.

Over the wires of many services, news filtered fitfully. Jaroslav Seifert, the Czech poet, had been awarded the Nobel Prize for Literature, a prize worth in cash terms some $190,000. Alas! The Nobel poet was all of eighty-three years old (echoing perhaps Goneril's criticism of Lear: I gave you all, and in good time) and was being shuttled from hospital to hospital, where the best readers were in too much pain to read and had retreated into indifference. When the poet's wife had learned about the award, she said, "Had it only come twenty years earlier."

Yes. How correct she was. Had everything in life—everything!—only arrived twenty years earlier.

Dear Sirs:

I should like to point out to you a mistranslation in the King James Version of the Old Testament. Chapter One of Genesis should read: In the beginning, God created the Heavens and the Earth. And God said let there be Life, and let that Life be fair.

Can that passage be translated in any other manner? I think not. Now that I have your attention, may I point out your TV series "Squat, Scum, and Litter" is . . .

ETC.

Howard De Kruif typed a few more letters. The alpha to omega of servile begging. He applied for teaching positions that did not exist, thus giving his enemies more weapons to lay him low, more fuel to burn him with. Dear Ichabod Bliss. Could you please consider . . . He could not get the tone right. He could not get the tone right because he knew there were no jobs waiting.

Dear Hunking Wentworth. Etc. He labored mightily in a country that did not value its children. He did not get the tone right because, even if there had been jobs waiting, an unlikely prospect at best, those would not be the jobs he truly desired. Everyone wanted a living soul for fifty cents an hour. The head of a fly-by-night small-town juiced-up-to-the-ass-with-comma-splices English department had told his friend Joan, "This is a part-time job, but we expect a full-time commitment." He had imagined what he would have done at such an interview. Pick up the desk and turn it over. "You fucking sonuvabitch, how can you talk to people like that? If you want a full-time commitment, then pay full time for it. Don't fuck around with people's lives as if they were some kind of scum, and you the Simon Legree of nontenured tracks!" Kick the chairman's teeth in would be a good way to do it, to be dragged out kicking and screaming. Smash their faces in. Make them pay for their stupidity and their arrogance. "You want a full-time commitment? I'll give you a full-time commitment! Right in the groin, I give it." They, so used to civilized behavior, yet ready to stab their colleagues in the back for a hundred-dollar-a-year raise.

Of course, he couldn't get the tone right, because he despised being on the begging end of existence, though, in the end, everyone seemed to be begging for the same thing. Someone had money and he did not. Thus, Howard's true work, his fine-honed labor, boiled down to one saintly act: to figure out how to transfer money out of one person's pocket into his own. Indeed, he could not sit still for ten minutes without worrying about money. Who had it. Who didn't. Who was never going to get it. You could make a killing, but you couldn't make a living. Write that in large letters.

He couldn't get the tone right, because, all in all, he despised the people at the other end, the ones who dispensed candy-ass favors, nickel and diming underlings to perdition, the lackluster tenured ones who had turned their backs on those less fortunate than themselves, each full-professor of them, eager to pounce on an infinity of split infinitives, mixed metaphors, and spelling errors up the old wahzoo. After the Seventh Day, what did God say to His divine creatures? "Life is only a part-time gig, but I expect a full-time commitment."

No wonder the snake in the garden got its way. What did the snake look like before it crawled on its belly in the dust?

"Daddy, tell me a story," Dora, dumb Dora, his youngest daughter, pleaded, as she, clad in baby-blue peacock-eyed pajamas and carrying her teddy bear by its fat left leg, entered his writing room and stood patiently next to his right elbow, her big blue eyes pleading for attention, as he himself was pleading for attention. Who was going to give anybody any attention? If attention had only come twenty years earlier! *Twenty Years Before the Missed.*

"All right," Howard said. "I'll tell you the story of a sea captain with a peg leg, who said to his crew as they were chasing the white whale of Fame and Fortune, 'Whaling is only a part-time job, but I expect a full-time commitment.'"

"No, tell me a real story, Daddy."

"I can't, kid. Real stories would break your heart. Besides," he added, swiveling in his chair and lifting her from the floor, the dumb floor, high into the air, the dumb air, "it is a real story. Who are you to know the difference between a real story and a false one? Are you planning to be a critic, kid? Or how about a teacher of freshman comp forever?"

"No, it's not." Dora, dumb Dora, was not to be fooled.

"There was a poet named Byron," Howard began, releasing his daughter to the floor, the dumb floor. "And, in one of his poems, *Childe Harold,* to be specific, Mr. Byron upset the universe by writing, 'To slowly trace the forest's changing scene.' What he should have written, of course, as anybody who is well educated can tell you, is 'To trace slowly the forest's changing scene.' And then he would have passed the muster of modest academic types and he would have lived happily ever after."

Dora pouted her dumb pout. Then stuck out her tongue. She was not loved any more because there were new lives on the way. Perhaps that is what she felt. Howard often felt the same way.

"I'm sorry, honey. I've got to go to meet Howard."

"You're Howard."

"Another Howard. My agent. Mack. You remember him."

Dora shook her head. Her thumb was in her mouth.

"I just have to put more books into boxes. You can help me if you want." That's right, put the kid to work early. "You've been freeloading off me long enough. Free meals. Free place to stay. What more do you want?" Howard's study had to be cleaned out to make room for the nursery. "It is with much regret that I inform you of the unhappy fate of the *Hawk Cutter. . . .*"

Dora helped by bringing him a solitary paperback.

Books he had collected over three decades or, to be more accurate, books that had collected him were stacked on the floor or had been tossed every which way into cardboard boxes. My kingdom for a good cardboard box!

The Death of the Moth and Other Essays
The World Almanac
Contemporary American Poets
The Holy Bible
The Holy World Almanac
The Holy Contemporary Poets
Lippincott's Pronouncing Biographical Dictionary
Great Modern Short Biographies of Holy Agents

Etc.

So many lives like his own. So many lives unlike his own. How could one ever tell the players without a scorecard? The scorecard of his life. A *New York Yankees Yearbook* caught sliding. Out! Out it went. You went to baseball games and thought: You sonsuvabitches! You're getting paid and I'm not!

Books by the hundreds. The thousands. The tens of thousands. Millions. Carted off to thrift shops and local libraries. Handed out to vagrants on the street so they could sell them or trade them for a cup of coffee. Thank God for libraries. It was a place to go when you were out of work. Even the courts upheld the rights of the homeless.

Of course, it was difficult to know what to do about books written by friends. You sent books to friends, and other writers sent their books to you. Any book by a friend had to be kept, packed, moved, stored; otherwise, it would be an act of betrayal. Howard had remembered his own hurt, his own astonishment, his own chagrin—as if he could remember anybody else's—when he had wandered into the holy Strand and had discovered in the sales bin his own book, one he had so thoughtfully inscribed to another writer, a friend of sorts.

But what vanity of vanities! An inscription in a book did not render it holy. Especially if the book was not worth reading in the first place. Inscriptions merely created an extra hazard, one more object to infringe on the space of the living. One more object made, because of the writing on the flyleaf, more difficult to sell. Almost impossible to give away. Collectors paid good money for the signatures of the famous. They did not pay for signatures of the hoi polloi, the atmosphere people, the professional part-timers.

Howard was not a superstar. That much had been driven home to him time and again, more than once had reduced his ego to ashes. Twenty years earlier a hot-shot editor at a hot-shot publishing house had written to him, saying, "We have so many superstars on our list that a good young writer doesn't stand much of a chance with us."

"Daddy, Mathilde's caught a moth," Dora announced, referring to her older sister.

"I don't give a shit," Howard said. "Just don't tell on your sister."

Dear Princess Di:

If you and the Prince are considering another child—in the hope of repairing your marriage—I hope you might consider some of the following names for the royal infant. The names do not necessarily recall the glories of Greece or the grandeur of Rome (it can never be the other way round), but the names may remind us of our common Puritan stock:

Eber Eager	Ichabod Bliss
Eliphalet Loud	Hunking Wentworth
Epaphroditus Chapman	Independence Whipple
Finis Gookin	Icybinda Wheelock
Fisco Shailer	

ETC.

You're going to have to think about making money, his agent said.

That evening Howard sat in the lounge of the Algonquin, the guest of Howard Mack of Mack and Welleck, high-rollers in the world of television and film. Mack, white-haired and energetic, was unusually nervous because he was bothered by a drooping eyelid. His doctors considered it to be a symptom of something more serious. Nearing sixty, he was beginning to take on a variety of exotic and nonexotic ailments. Perhaps his gay life-style was catching up to him.

"It's writers," he joked. "You're giving me ulcers and making me sick."

The two Howards were friends of sorts. That was the hazy part of the author-agent relationship. They were friendly co-workers, but neither had ever been in the other's apartment. They were also each other's client, though, for the fifteen years Howard had been with Mack, the agent had overpowered the writer. He had the stronger hand.

I must not appear to need anything, Howard thought. I must appear free from want. Free from need. Free from hurt. It's just a couple of high-priced drinks on the house. Casual as hell.

Three years later Mack would be dead from AIDS.

But tonight every small round table in the lounge was surrounded by theater-going men and women of advanced middle-age. The ghosts of the Round Table laughed merrily. Mack himself was on the way to the theater. Some hot-shot Italian actor was in town with a one-man show. "The reason I'm going," Mack announced, "is because Shelley Winters is going. She's going to be in the audience and everybody's going to be watching her. She's certainly going to be a lot more interesting than anything that will happen on the stage." He laughed, ordered another round of Bloody Marys.

Howard tried to think of a clever retort, but none came to mind. All he wanted was a list of names, some new contacts so he could go sell himself to the highest bidder, but he didn't know how to raise the subject gracefully. And so he drank. Besides, the request could not be graceful. The high-rollers had to come to you. If you had to go to them, you were already a loser. Just like mail was for losers. If they wanted you, they'd call.

A skeleton-like old woman carrying two heavy shopping bags entered the lobby and began to curse the waiters. "You bastards!" she cried. "This is my hotel! It belongs to me. I can sit anywhere I goddamn like." The woman was quietly and efficiently escorted to the street. Few people looked up for more than a moment. Those who did were out-of-towners.

Mack blithely trotted out an anecdote about three women desperate to get married. Zippi-dee-doo-dah. The great thing about Mack was that nothing bothered him. He had the emotional involvement of a clam.

A pirate movie. Yes, the time was ripe for a pirate movie. An allegory for our times. Lower your jib. Dumb drunk.

Faversham. February 8, 1781

Gentlemen:

It is with much regret that I inform you of the unhappy fate of the *Hawk Cutter* under my command. We weighed anchor, and proceeded to sea on Monday the 7th, and in the evening descried a sail, bearing W.S.W. to which he gave chase (to Windward) she at the same time pursuing us; and at about 8 in the evening came up with each other. . . .

"A book for a musical," Mack said. "That's what I want you to think about. When I think of a musical, I think of something colorful, flashy, easy to follow. Pizzazz. Lots of dancers."

"What about our friend at NBC?" Howard asked. "She always liked my work."

"She doesn't work there anymore," the agent said. "Besides they're not buying the kind of stuff you're writing."

"I guess that's true," Howard said, signaling for the waiter. What should he have said? My study's going to be changed into a nursery? "I can't argue with that." Suppose he were delivered a hand grenade on a silver tray. Whom should he destroy? Not even a hand grenade would reach Mack. He was an island unto himself. Who knew what he cared about? Ask him something trivial about the movies; Mack would love that. Or the poor, lazy people of Morocco, whom Mack hated.

"Look," Mack said. "I want you to stop being afraid."

"Afraid?"

"I can tell."

"Can you?"

Mack nodded. "I want you to clear everything from your mind." He waved his hand like a mad magician. "Have you cleared everything from your mind?"

Howard smiled.

"Don't smile or I won't do it. Have you cleared everything from your mind?"

Howard nodded. Nothing remained in his head but the *Hawk Cutter* and another ancient letter going to the Dead Letter Office of Missed Opportunities.

Mack pulled a pair of black-rimmed glasses from his jacket pocket and put them on. He leaned forward in his chair. Through the well-polished revolving doors, a woman entered who looked exactly like Shelley Winters. "I want you to picture yourself walking down a road," Mack told him. "What kind of road are you walking down?"

Not the straight and narrow, Howard thought. He said: "A dusty road. A long, dusty road. Every time I take a step, great clouds of dust fly up behind me."

"A dusty road?" Mack repeated. "Anything on either side of the road?"

"Nothing on either side. Just a flat, bare landscape."

"Maybe some grass?" his agent prompted. "A few trees?"

Howard nodded. He was nothing if not agreeable. Howard's

previous agent had once fallen asleep during the opening night of one of Howard's plays. Howard had never forgotten that. Nor forgiven. "A few trees."

"Now this road is leading to a house. What kind of a house do you see?" "I see a simple white wooden house. It has a fence around it. A white wooden picket fence. The kind of fence that Tom Sawyer would have been hired to whitewash."

"OK," the agent continued. "There's a fence around the house. I take it there's a gate in the fence?" Mack leaned forward, but his voice seemed to be growing colder. Or maybe it was the air-conditioning. Forty-four years old and Howard had never lived in a house with air-conditioning. As one grew older, creature comforts took on greater weight.

Howard agreed. "Yes. There's a gate."

"Now you go through the gate." Was Mack asking him or ordering him? Howard could not be certain. Too many subtle and unsubtle negotiations. If Howard would only sleep with him. . . .

"I go through the gate."

"Does this house have a front porch?"

"Yes. There is a huge front porch."

"OK." Mack pushed his eyeglasses down to the end of his nose and peered over them. "Go up the front porch, cross the porch, and approach the front door. Are you doing that?"

"Yes."

"Open the front door and enter the house."

"Is the house locked?" Howard asked.

"No. The house isn't locked. Just open the door. Now you are inside the house. What do you see?"

Must see a telephone, Howard thought. One out of two households, etc. "I enter the house," Howard answered, reaching for his drink, "and I see a table with a candle on it." Change that, he thought. Maybe I'm getting too phallic. "There's a moth fluttering around the candle-flame. There's a fire in the fireplace."

"Well, a fire in the fireplace," Mack said, pushing his glasses back. "That should make the room nice and cozy. What do you do in this room?"

"Actually I don't do anything in the room," Howard replied, smiling.

"Nothing?"

"No, I just cross the room and go upstairs."

Mack grimaced. "I didn't realize that this house had an upstairs to it."

"It does." Fuck him. It's my house.

"OK. You go upstairs. Where do you go?"

"I go to the bedroom."

"Where is the bedroom?"

At last. A subject he's interested in. "There's a bedroom at the top of the stairs. I enter the bedroom."

"Anybody in the bedroom?"

The waiter delivered a third round of Bloody Marys. "Nobody in the bedroom."

"All right. You're in the bedroom all by yourself. There's a closet in this bedroom. I want you to go to the closet and open it. What's inside the closet?"

"A monster. There's a monster in the closet," Howard said, smirking.

"Well, let the monster out!" Mack shouted. Several people turned to look. Howard blushed. Mack pulled out his thick black wallet. "That monster is your fear. Don't you see? Now you see it. Now that you can see your fear, you can control it! There it is. In your room. In your house. The monster in the closet. Just tame it. Contain it."

Mack quickly paid the bill, and he and Howard left the hotel.

Back home, in the bedroom with its single closet, while Mack was devouring the night life of the city, Howard's wife, Paula, asked him about the meeting. "Did Howard say anything about getting you a job?"

"No," Howard answered, his lips tight. "Nobody's buying right now." He paused at the closet door, reached forward to open it, then changed his mind. After all, it wasn't his closet. Better he should go and check on his sleeping daughters. "Everybody's waiting for an upturn in the economy."

"You didn't tell him that he should be getting you more work?"

"No." My daughters, he thought, are you dreaming of pirates, of moths, of tiny white-fenced houses, etc.?

ETC.?

about
the
author

Born in Massachusetts in 1942, Louis Phillips is the author of more than thirty books for children and adults, and his poems, plays, and stories have appeared in such publications as the *Georgia Review, Massachusetts Review, Hawaii Review,* and the *Nassau Review*. His book of poems, *The Time, the Hour, the Solitariness of the Place,* was the co-winner of the Swallow's Tale poetry contest and was published by that press in 1985. His plays have been performed in New York City and in regional theaters throughout the United States. Phillips was an NEA Fellow in Playwrighting in 1981 and a Regents Fellow in Playwrighting at the University of California, San Diego. He currently lives with his wife and twin sons in Manhattan, where he teaches creative writing at the School of Visual Arts.